PAID IN BLOOD

PAID IN BLOOD

WATCHDOGS OF THE VEIL™ BOOK ONE

MICHAEL ANDERLE

DON'T MISS OUR NEW RELEASES

Join the LMBPN email list to be notified of new releases and special promotions (which happen often) by following this link:

http://lmbpn.com/email/

Cover Art by Jake @ J Caleb Design
http://jcalebdesign.com / jcalebdesign@gmail.com

A Michael Anderle Production

LMBPN Publishing
PMB 196, 2540 South Maryland Pkwy
Las Vegas, NV 89109

Version 1.01, April 2023
eBook ISBN: 979-8-88878-281-1
Print ISBN: 979-8-88878-282-8

THE PAID IN BLOOD TEAM

Thanks to our Beta Team
David Laughlin, Kelly O'Donnell, Rachel Beckford,
Malyssa Brannon

Thanks to the JIT Readers

Zacc Pelter
Dave Hicks
Peter Manis
Diane L. Smith
Dorothy Lloyd
Jeff Goode
Jackey Hankard-Brodie
Christopher Gilliard
Paul Westman
Jan Hunnicutt

Editor
The SkyFyre Editing Team

CHAPTER ONE

Carlton Priez Pierce smiled good-naturedly at the polygraph examiner for the Miami FBI. "We all done here?"

"Yes. You're done." The man did not smile back. Polygraph examiners generally didn't. He merely looked at Carlton with that bland FBI professionalism that didn't communicate if you were in trouble.

He felt like he was going to be sick, but he didn't show it. He'd felt that way throughout the entire interview, but the techniques they'd taught him really worked. He'd passed with flying colors despite his nausea.

"All right then. Thanks, man. I'll see myself out."

The polygraph examiner didn't reply, just bent over his work.

The painful roiling in his stomach was only natural. He was hoping to get a job with the Federal Bureau of Investigation, and to do that, you had to pass a lie detector test. That was a challenge, even with the pristine background he'd purchased.

That background painted him as someone else, not the man who'd been coerced into working for the CIA. It also hid his gang membership by making him a younger man.

His contact had said putting it together had been tricky but not impossible, and they were sure it would hold up against the high-level scrutiny it would be exposed to. The fact that he'd never been arrested in his time as a gang member had made it easier.

Of course, that left the onus on him to make the most of his CIA training to keep the facts to himself and avoid getting caught.

Carlton left the examination room, and a blonde woman in a blue suit and skirt ensemble smiled pleasantly at him. "So, that part's done. Nobody's thrilled about taking a polygraph, but it's better to get it out of the way."

"Yeah, that makes sense. What's next?"

"I expect we'll be reaching out to you soon. The next step in the process is a panel interview with some of our field agents. They're generally good at spotting who's a good fit for this type of work."

Carlton knew that, but he listened eagerly. "I'm looking forward to it. Thanks for everything!"

She smiled in response and wished him a good afternoon. He stepped out of the FBI offices and headed out into the Miami heat, then tugged down his tie and pulled his shirt collar open.

The FBI's Miami headquarters was a slick new building located in the suburb of Miramar. A food truck was parked out front, selling slow-cooked brisket sandwiches to FBI employees on their lunch breaks. Carlton stopped at the window.

"Hey, man. I know this truck. You guys swing by my neighborhood all the time."

The man in the truck took a long look at his face and then nodded. "Yeah, I seen you around. You want a brisket sandwich, man?"

"Not today. I'm headed home, but if I get this job, I'll eat here all the time!"

"Good luck on the job, man."

He would have gone ahead and ordered a brisket sandwich if not for the painful acidic feeling in his stomach. He had to get a handle on his anxiety before he could eat anything.

It wasn't only the test that had taken him there. The heavens knew he'd faced that level of stress before, but not for this long.

A few months, even a couple of years, but this last round of pressure had lasted much longer than that and was made harder because not only had he been dodging his previous employers, but also the criminal elements they'd alerted to his continued existence.

Then there was the consternation caused by his ex.

These thoughts occupied Carlton as he strolled into the visitor parking lot. He methodically worked through the process he used to control his anxiety.

"It's okay," he told himself. "There's no reason to be nervous. Just answer the questions."

Carlton had developed the questions over a period of several years. He'd been through a lot of stressful and dangerous situations in his life, starting with his juvenile involvement in the gang and continuing through the work he'd done for the CIA.

He'd often faced overwhelming stress and fear, and in situations like that, he asked himself certain questions. What he'd discovered over time was that the questions really helped. If you asked them methodically and answered them truthfully, you could get a handle on the most terrifying situations a man could ever find himself in.

Question Number One: What am I afraid of?

He was afraid that they would somehow find out he was a former gang member turned CIA operative who was trying to go straight and get a job with the FBI. The reality was that he looked legitimate for a former gang member.

He had no tattoos, no bullet wounds, and no criminal record. He'd never been caught for anything; he'd never even been arrested. There hadn't been anything for the specialist working on his new ID to chase down and expunge.

As a CIA operative, he'd worked mostly in South America, and while there was a paper trail, the new identity wasn't connected. He'd thought about having the paper trail scrubbed, but since he didn't think he'd ever be going back that way, it worked as a form of misdirection.

Anyone who knew his CIA identity could follow it south all they wanted. The trail would take them far away from where his current persona existed and reduce the chances of anyone hunting him from accidentally stumbling over him.

The "case of mistaken identity" cover was easier to enact if his former self had never been connected with places his current self now haunted.

Question Number Two: What could go wrong to make that fear a reality? With all the lying he had done, both on paper and face to face, it was quite possible they'd find something in his story that didn't add up. If that occurred, one of two bad things could happen.

They could lock him up for fraud, or they could dig too deep in trying to uncover the truth about him. If they dug too deep, who knows what the CIA might do to cover up his involvement with them? Some of what he'd done for them in South America was not suitable for public consumption.

The irony was that he wasn't a bad man. Sure, as a former criminal and Agency spook, he had a shady past. Still, he would never have chosen any of it for himself if he'd had any choice.

He didn't choose the gang but had been born into it. In a neighborhood where gang members were often third generation, the remarkable thing wasn't that he'd joined but that he'd chosen to leave. As for the CIA, they'd used him for their own purposes. Their recruitment methods had been closer to blackmail than anything else, and he'd gotten out of that life as quickly as he could.

Now, all he wanted was to use his skills to do some good in the world while making a living and getting back to the ones he loved. If he went inside, whether for fraud or anything else, there was a chance that someone he knew from his old life could be in there with him.

Hell, someone he'd known through his Agency work could be in there, especially if he did time here in Florida. If anyone recognized him, they could snitch on him for something if they didn't try to kill him. It all depended on which faction they were part of.

Random people trying to kill him was not much of a

threat in and of itself. He could handle himself, but it would draw more attention to him while he was locked up, and that was not a good thing.

As he got into his car and clicked the seatbelt, Carlton asked the next question in his process.

Question Number Three: What can I do to prevent this from happening?

Apart from disappearing into the west, there was nothing he *could* do. He was so deep into this charade that if they were going to catch him, they already had what they needed to do so.

If he stayed, he would either come out of this process as a *bona fide* FBI field agent or locked up for lying to the government. It was a hell of a gamble, but with the risk came a hell of a payoff.

Running wasn't an option anyway. Before he started up his car, Carlton pulled out his wallet and looked at the only copy of a picture he had taken nearly five years ago—a picture of a dark-haired young woman with the bronze complexion and distinct features of the Chehalis people, Washington's "People of the Sands."

The young woman in the picture was sitting on a couch and holding a baby boy. The photo was blurred because it was taken from outside the trailer they were in and from some distance away. He'd had a fling with her while hiding on the Confederated Tribes of the Chehalis Reservation after a particularly messy situation with the CIA. The baby was his son, Tuula-hwip or "Tully," even though the child did not know he was the father, and the young woman did not acknowledge it.

Carlton looked at them both with loss and yearning in

his eyes, then closed his wallet and put it back in his pocket before starting his car. If there was one thing he knew, it was that the young woman in the photo—Marla "Marly" Lusk—would not let him have anything to do with his son if he wasn't legitimate.

That was why he was here. He had followed her to Miami when she came here on a grant from the University of Miami to participate in an educational program for mothers with young children. She would be here for a few years, which gave him a chance to get the FBI gig, earn a good solid income, and build a trustworthy reputation.

Maybe then she would no longer think of him as a shady character she should never have trusted. Maybe then she would let him back into her life as well as Tully's. When they eventually went back to the Chehalis reservation, which Marly was hoping to do as a social worker and trauma counselor, he could put in for a transfer to the Seattle office.

Even if they gave him the transfer, it would be a hell of a commute. An hour and a half, depending on traffic, but he would be able to build a life with the two people he loved.

That was his crazy and likely suicidal plan, created out of pure desperation when he'd learned he had a son. As far as Marly was concerned, he had been a bad decision. A questionable character she'd had a fling with. She'd had a son as a result, but that didn't make him the boy's father in her eyes.

To earn his way back into her life, he would have to demonstrate that he was capable of something more. Something that would cancel or at least balance the less wholesome aspects of his past. This crazy FBI plan might do that. How did you prove that you were one of the good guys? By transforming yourself into one of the good guys.

Pulling out onto the highway, Carlton Priez Pierce clenched his jaw. Like it always did, that photo had reminded him of what he was working toward. It had reminded him of his mission. There was nothing he could do but stay the course, so that was what he would do. Working his way through the Miami traffic, the FBI's most unlikely recruit drove back to his apartment.

Carlton was at his own place barely long enough to change out of his interview clothes and go for a jog along the beach before hitting an outdoor gym nearby. It was a relatively quiet night, and the few other people who were there drifted away one by one.

Before he knew it, he was alone at the gym, muscles burning as he put himself through the paces. He was working out on the heavy bag, repeating a vicious string of combinations over and over.

"Lookin' a little angry, there, big guy. Rough day at work?"

He looked around when he heard those words and found a cute blonde grinning at him as she started her workout. She had a strong Southern drawl, and her blue eyes sparkled with laughter.

"Uh, sorry about that," he replied. "I'll try to keep it a little more…sane."

She laughed, putting a hand over her mouth. "Don't

take it personal. You look like Jason Bourne or somethin'. You know, trainin' to be a deadly CIA killer."

His blood ran cold, but when he looked into her eyes, he realized she didn't know a thing. She was only being friendly. Maybe even flirting.

He decided the conversation needed diversion. Anyone who knew his history would have known he'd learned this combo in the CIA or maybe his gang days, but that wasn't really true. It would be best if no one believed he'd been anywhere near either.

"Oh, that's not it," he told her. He kept working the combo as he talked, taking the intensity down enough to allow for conversation. "I saw this documentary, you know? I thought I'd change up my game."

"Oh, really?" she replied, her eyebrows raising. She was lifting bright blue dumbbells as they talked. "Well, it looks just like one of the workouts they use in the movies."

"Yeah? Then maybe it's a good workout. I'm sure it's not used by anyone working in that area."

He wasn't, but if he sounded boring, maybe she'd go away.

"Those guys who have to kill people, I'm sure those guys would work out like that. You *sure* you're not like one of those?" Her tone was light and on the friendly side of flirty. To her, the conversation was a joke, a mildly titillating chat about CIA hitmen.

Carlton shook his head. "Not even close."

"Well, you could have fooled me." She took a different tack. "How do you think they go about killing someone, then? That has to be hard."

"Who knows? Maybe they're like crocodiles and lie in wait for their target to come along."

She thought about that for a minute. It seemed to Carlton like she was trying to decide whether to take this conversation further. It didn't matter since he wasn't trying to get anywhere with her. He was blowing off steam and hoping she'd go away before someone overheard them and took a closer look at him.

"I'm pretty patient," she commented at last. "Think I should apply to work for the CIA?"

"Depends on how much of a crocodile you think you can be."

"I'm sure you have to be more than that, right?"

"Maybe." Carlton tried being noncommittal, but she didn't take the hint.

"See? There is! Well, what is it, then, Mr. Mysterious Intense Guy?"

Carlton couldn't help grinning, amused by the thought that she would remember him as Mr. Mysterious Intense Guy. Little did she know how right she was.

"How would I know? I think as well as being patient, you'd have to ask yourself if you could deal with the psychological consequences of killing someone."

"Huh. Well, I don't like the sound of psychological consequences. Maybe I'd better stick to my career as a dental technician."

He grinned at her. "That's a respectable line of work."

Her cell phone rang, and she picked it up and looked at the screen. With a pouty frown, she announced, "Ah, hell. It's my boyfriend. Just when I was startin' to have fun." She pressed the button and spoke. "Hey, baby. Yeah, just doin' a little workout. Oh, you are? Well, meet me out front then. Yeah. I'll see you soon!"

She hung up the phone and gave Carlton a big grin. "Well, it was fun talkin' to you, Mr. Mysterious Intense Guy. I think you're kinda fun."

He grinned in response and waved goodbye. He brought the intensity of his workout back up again as she walked away.

The conversation reminded him of the killers he'd met in his past. Most of them hadn't gone hunting.

They'd been just like crocodiles. They'd watched and waited someplace they knew the target would come to them. Usually someplace the target would be vulnerable.

Carlton was different, though. He'd survived for a long time under very dangerous conditions, and he hoped to continue doing so. As a result, he was militant about staying fit and ready to fight.

It only took one time misjudging your read as an operative, and the target could turn the tables. Even if you survived, you'd have incriminating scars or other injuries, provoking suspicions of criminal activity wherever you went.

Carlton made sure he could pull the job off clean no matter what happened. No injuries, no collateral damage, no mess of any kind. As a CIA agent, he'd been a ghost.

He was good at his work, but it was a lonely existence, and he resented that he'd been pressured into it. Not only that, but it would never let him have a normal life or a normal relationship.

That had been fine for a time. He'd made his peace with it until he found out about his son. That was when something fundamental, foundational, primal changed inside him. So here he was in Miami, trying to become one of the good guys after a lifetime of being a not-so-good guy.

That was why he was taking these crazy risks. It got to him, though, and that was why Carlton was working this combination on the heavy bag over and over.

It was all about pouring his anxiety, his anger, and yes, even his fear into the bag, so it didn't remain inside his body. He kept swinging until he had nothing left to give. Until he staggered back from the swinging heavy bag, panting loudly with the effort.

Someone clapped slowly and deliberately, and it was clearly directed at him. He looked around, wondering why someone was paying attention to him, never mind being sarcastic.

His eyes fell on a tall, well-dressed woman with dark hair and pale skin standing at the edge of the gym. He had the distinct impression that her applause was mocking, but he managed to control his pugnacious urge to posture.

Instead, he adopted an affable and self-deprecating demeanor. With a seemingly amused smile, he nodded in her direction. "Thank you for the applause. I'll be here all week."

The woman's only reply was a cool and self-controlled smile. She stayed where she was as if she was waiting for something, as Carlton toweled off. It was only when he started to leave that she moved to intercept him.

The way she moved reminded Carlton of a jungle cat—strong, agile, and, more than anything, confident. As a reformed predator, he could scent a dangerous person from across the room, and this woman qualified. His senses were on high alert as she approached, but there was something different about her.

It wasn't a swagger but a sharpness. Professionalism. You only found that with the best in private business or government. It brought him up short, and he couldn't help looking around to see if agents were moving in around him.

This is it, isn't it? They've caught me.

Not only in his lies but everything else. Hadn't the old-timers in the gang always told him that if the FBI wanted to catch you, they would? Cops were one thing, but the FBI was like a vengeful god. And what had he done?

He'd walked right up and pissed on the altar with his lies disguised as offerings! He could see it now; agents swarming in from every direction, drawing their guns as they ran in. He could run, but they'd have every escape route blocked.

They'd tackle him from behind, put him on the ground face-first, and stick a knee in the small of his back. He wouldn't see blue sky again for years, except for an hour a day in the prison exercise yard.

The urge to bolt was almost overpowering, though he already knew it would not work. His well-honed instincts shouted, "Ambush!" even though he didn't see any agents.

Was she an assassin rather than an FBI agent? No. If she was an assassin, he would never have seen her coming. She would have hovered in the background, inconspicuous, an ambush predator, and when he wasn't looking, she would have shot him in the head.

He was ready to run, but he couldn't tell what he was running from. Therefore, he didn't do anything.

The woman spoke for the first time. "You know, for a man looking for a job, you sure look like you are about to run off."

Carlton looked at her uncertainly. "What do you mean, ma'am?"

The woman smiled, but her smile was as distant and cool as her tone of voice. "I mean, for someone looking to join the FBI, you look awfully nervous. That makes me wonder why. Do you have something to hide?"

Trying to control his pounding heartbeat, Carlton assessed the situation.

Was this a test?

"Do you work for the Bureau, ma'am?"

Her voice was slick and self-controlled. "I've been sent to do an independent verification. All your neighbors and acquaintances have been checked, and they're all big fans. Especially given that they've only known you for less than a decade."

"Less than a decade?" He raised his eyebrows. "That doesn't seem like a short time."

"Less than a decade between all of them combined."

Carlton could feel the noose tightening. "I'm not sure what you mean."

The woman's voice went from cool to cold. "Let's not start this relationship with lies, shall we? The point is that certain...discrepancies have emerged in your background. These discrepancies prompted further investigation, and that investigation revealed all sorts of interesting tidbits about your past recreational activities and your past employers."

She knew about both his past criminal history *and* his

past history with the CIA? How could she possibly have learned all that? His new ID was impeccable. *Impeccable!*

He should know. He'd not only bought the best, but he'd had it pen-tested *by* the best, and *they* hadn't been able to crack it. Now he was broke, but it had been a small price to pay for his continued safety.

Carlton was still looking to run, but he couldn't shake the feeling that there'd be someone waiting for him whichever way he went. "Are these accusations attached to any charges?"

The woman raised her eyebrows. "Charges? No. But there could be an offer for you if you stop looking to rabbit."

Carlton was caught off-guard. "An offer? What sort of offer?"

"You knew what was going to happen next in your application to the Bureau?" she asked.

Carlton nodded. "Yeah. I mean, yes, ma'am. A panel interview with field agents to see how well I might work with the team here in Miami."

The woman smiled enigmatically. "Bingo. We've got another field-based test for you instead. It will seem...unconventional, but you are an unconventional candidate, so perhaps that's not so surprising."

Carlton didn't know how to take that. He wasn't sure she worked for the FBI. "And if I refuse?"

"Well, you're not going to be an FBI agent, that is for sure. Hell, they wouldn't even trust you to take out the trash, not after you beat their polygraph test like you were going to a picnic. Once the wheels of bureaucracy catch up with you, you'll probably find yourself working with the government, but that won't be what you've been hoping for. At best, you'll have to become a professional snitch. At worst, you'll be making license plates. Either way, it will only last long enough for one of your former associates to find you and put something sharp someplace uncomfortable."

Carlton lowered his head. This was what had happened when the CIA recruited him. "I don't have a choice, then?"

The woman's voice dripped with fake friendliness. "Oh, honey, you certainly do. You can run, you can stay and wait, or you can take my offer. It's all your choice. That's the one thing I'm not going to take away from you. I'm not a monster."

The way she said that last part made Carlton uncomfortable, but he couldn't put his finger on why. Maybe it was that she felt monstrous, whatever that meant. "I never caught your name, ma'am?"

"That's because I didn't drop it, darling, but for now, you can call me Mabel."

"Agent Mabel? Special Agent Mabel? Director Mabel?" Carlton was trying to get a handle on who she was, how much authority she had, and what she could do to him.

The woman's smile was like a block of ice. "Just Mabel, sweetie. Why are you so concerned about what to call me?"

He didn't have a choice for now. As long as he could stay alive, he could figure out some way to get out of this later, assuming that seemed like a good idea. "I'm interested in hearing more."

"I'm glad to hear it," she replied and turned to walk down the beach. "Come on. We've got a short drive before we get on with the next phase of your application."

CHAPTER TWO

Mabel's car was a nice but not ostentatious sedan. They got in, and she drove them into a section of Miami not found on any tourist brochure.

It started subtly. He noticed the disappearance of restaurants. Then they were in a neighborhood with no food markets, just the occasional liquor store with barred windows and armed guards out front.

There were crumbling buildings and boarded-up businesses, the products of poverty and urban decay. Gang graffiti covered every surface, reminding Carlton of where he came from. He even recognized some of the gangs from home, although the individual sets were different. Others were unfamiliar and most likely unique to Miami.

As they drove on, Carlton tried to prepare himself for what might be asked. At first, he thought of it as a hazing ritual, the functional equivalent of getting "jumped in" to a gang.

He paused, thinking he didn't know this woman or

anything about her. He didn't even know if she was from the Bureau.

He started thinking. Was she FBI, or was she with a government shadow agency?

God knows I encountered that shit in my days with the CIA.

He'd run across men and women who made his skin crawl a few times in his previous career. He couldn't identify them as working for any specific agency. They didn't seem to exist except that he'd met them. In other words, spooks.

That made him feel he was going in the opposite direction from where he wanted to go. Instead of being a good guy, he was sure he was about to become a bad guy for the government.

If there was something worse than lying in wait for a target and taking him out of the world discreetly, he was about to find out.

At the same time, a solid government job wouldn't be so bad. If they gave him the right cover identity, he'd be able to say he worked for the government without lying. That wouldn't sound bad when he talked to Marly.

As long as he did a good job, they would take good care of him. That seemed to be the case for the spooks he'd occasionally encountered while working for the CIA. He didn't appreciate being pressured, but perhaps there was some way he could turn this to his advantage.

If he wanted to get back to Marly and Tully, a little flexibility might be in order.

"What are you thinking about?" Mabel asked him.

"What you said about choices," he answered.

No matter what Mabel had said, he *didn't* have a choice.

If he didn't do whatever she asked him to, he didn't think he'd ever see Marly or Tully again. He didn't know how it would play out, but the feds, or whoever Mabel worked for, had him dead to rights.

He was determined to build a bridge to Marly and Tully. His original plan, as crazy as it had been, was to build that bridge with an FBI position. If he had to build it with the corpses of enemies of the State instead, then so be it. He had set his course, and he wasn't backing down. He'd lost too much time already.

"Choices," she said quietly. "You always have them. Even a man in a prison cell has them."

That didn't sound encouraging, so he left it. If this was a test, he intended to pass. Wherever they were going, he would go. Whatever he had to do, he would do. As long as it got him back to the people he loved, it was worth it.

Mabel looked at him. "Your face is grim. Lighten up. The world is a black joke, and you should laugh at it."

"I'll bear that in mind."

They pulled up to the most rundown building in what looked like the most rundown corner of Miami. At first glance, it might have been a machine shop or a small-scale industrial facility. Most of the place was boarded up, but one section had collapsed, blocking the entrance.

Mabel stopped the car but kept the engine running. "First things first. Get out and find a way inside that building while I find us a parking space."

Finding a way inside did not look easy, but Carlton stepped out of the car, glancing around for threats. He stood in front of the building and knew the sudden sensation of cold had nothing to do with the night air. It was as hot and muggy as ever, so this was something else.

He had felt it before as a gangbanger. On the street, you sometimes had to go through abandoned buildings and hide in different random places, and sometimes you'd find yourself in a place where things just seemed wrong. You couldn't say why, but there was something about the place that gave you the creeps. This building was one of those.

He avoided such places when he could, but it wasn't always possible. When he was inside one, he wasn't able to shake the feeling something was off and unnatural. It was frightening on a level unlike anything else.

It was a weird sensation and felt like going back in time to his younger days. He remembered crouching in the dark with a Nine in his hand and the hairs on the back of his neck standing up.

The weird thing was that nothing ever happened in those places. He was too much a creature of instinct to say it was all in his head, but he'd always made it through them unscathed.

There was no reason to think this place was any different. This was just a test and a juvenile one at that. Carlton steeled himself against the skin-crawling feeling and began to prowl the outside of the building.

The place seemed deserted. There were no empty beer cans or discarded cigarette packs. No sign that even a roach had scuttled by. The place was dirty and decrepit, and a lot of species liked nothing better, but there were no living things near it. Anything with any sense and the ability to move wouldn't come here.

What does that say about me?

He smiled grimly. Mabel was right; it was better to laugh at the world than let it get to you. He finally spotted a way in, a place where the rusted back of a filing cabinet was the only thing blocking a glassless window.

He bent to see if he could move it, and when he pushed, it gave a screeching scrape. The sound was painfully loud in the stillness of the night, but the cabinet moved. He had succeeded in finding a way in.

Carlton peered through the window, wondering if he should go inside. It was so dark in there that he couldn't see what kind of room it was. He felt something behind him and spun to find Mabel at his shoulder.

How the hell did she do that?

Carlton was shaken. He didn't know anyone capable of sneaking up on him and wouldn't have believed someone could get as close as she had before he became aware.

That was the main source of comfort to him when he thought about the CIA. If they sent anyone after him, that person would have to move damn quietly.

Mabel, however, had gotten right behind him before he noticed her presence. She was looking at him like a bird looking at a fat, tasty worm.

Hiding his shock and fear, Carlton tried to refocus on the task at hand. "I think I found a way in."

She smiled in that cool way, as if she knew exactly what made him so nervous and was quite amused. Carlton couldn't put his finger on it, but he had the feeling she was more than she seemed. Much more.

Mabel nodded. "Head on in."

It occurred to Carlton that this was the perfect place to

bring a person if you didn't want their corpse to be discovered.

He didn't see any weapons on Mabel, though, and he'd seen no evidence of anyone waiting inside the building. No, this was too elaborate a setup for an assassination attempt.

Doing his best to focus, keep his cool, and stay aware, Carlton went in through the glassless window. Mabel followed him.

Carlton had to be careful as he crawled through the opening in case there were jagged shards of glass. After he made it inside, he was surprised to see how easily Mabel came through. It was as if she had no fear of being cut. Maybe no fear of anything.

Carlton looked around. The only light was a dim glow from the buildings outside. Now that he thought about it, Carlton realized the streetlights in front of the building had all burned out.

It wasn't easy to see, but he could tell the place was as decayed and rundown as he'd believed. As he moved slowly through the room, he kept running into broken-down machines and other pieces of equipment that had been left to rust.

Before they'd become nondescript lumps, they might have fetched some cash. Why had no one come to take them? A desperate junkie could have gotten quite a few solid scores from this place before the Florida humidity wrecked everything inside.

It all added to the sense that this was a forbidden place. People stayed out of here. Stray cats stayed out of here. Even the city's most desperate junkies stayed out of here.

So, what am I *doing here?*

"What's, uh… What's the mission here, Mabel?"

"Nervous?" she asked in mocking tones. "Come on. Haven't you ever been in an abandoned building before?"

Was she really not feeling it? Carlton found that difficult to believe, but he didn't want to say anything in case it was only his imagination.

"Don't worry about it," she told him. "We're looking for a way into the basement."

"What are we doing in the basement?"

She didn't answer.

Once more, Carlton's warning sense prickled. He felt like he was walking into an enemy neighborhood—a place where you weren't safe, and you knew it.

If the wrong person saw you and understood who you were, you'd be killed, but at the same time, you had a chance.

Maybe no one from the enemy set was out and about. Maybe no one saw you. Maybe they saw you, but they didn't make you as a gang member.

That's what it felt like. Like he had a chance, but only if he was a hundred-percent alert and damned lucky too.

As he explored the rooms one by one, the sense of being in danger got worse. He kept finding evidence that there *was* activity here despite the powerful impression that nothing living ever came into the place.

If nothing came in, why did he keep finding disturbances in the dust as if someone had touched something? What were those stains in the far left corner that looked like bloodstains to his experienced eye?

There still didn't seem to be anyone here now, though.

He was alone, not counting Mabel, and Mabel didn't seem too keen on keeping an eye on him. She was wandering randomly through the darkness like he was, looking for the basement entrance.

Carlton's sharp senses and well-honed instincts led him to the right spot. He noticed a pile of random debris heaped in a corner, but when he looked closer, he found that it wasn't random. It seemed to have been heaped up recently, judging by the disturbed dust around it.

Under the rotting old two-by-fours and moist cardboard boxes, he found some abandoned equipment and pushed it aside to reveal a trapdoor beneath.

This has got to be it. Mabel should see this.

Leaving the trapdoor, he backtracked until he found her holding a crowbar to her nose. As far as he could tell, she was sniffing it like a flower or a perfume bottle.

Well, that's weird.

"I found a trapdoor in the floor."

She lowered the crowbar. "Okay, show me."

"It's in here." He led her to the basement access door and indicated the pile of debris and equipment with his hand. "It was hidden under all that."

She leaned in and looked down at the door, frowning. "Okay. Open it up."

Carlton bent and pulled on the handle, but it wouldn't budge. "It's locked."

"Here, use this crowbar."

It was the crowbar she'd been sniffing at a moment earlier. Carlton raised his eyebrows, and she shrugged.

"It's safe. I checked it."

Carlton didn't know what she meant by that. He was sure Mabel was messing with him, but...

In for a penny, in for a pound.

He took the crowbar and pried the trapdoor open, straining against the lock before it opened with a faint clink.

Once the door was open, Carlton saw a metal ladder bolted to the top of a shaft. He couldn't see the bottom, but the ladder descended into darkness.

Carlton frowned at it, but Mabel produced unusually potent glowsticks from her pockets. She dropped bundles of them into the darkness, and they fell like tiny little stars.

"Okay," she announced, "It's time to do this. I need you to head down there and find a book. A ledger, actually. Find it and bring it to me."

The hair stood up on the back of his neck. "You've got to be kidding."

She shook her head. "I'm not kidding."

"What is it, some forbidden tome bound in human skin and written in blood?"

"I doubt it. I expect it will look like a common office ledger, probably with a spiral spine. They sit open on a table better than ancient forbidden tomes usually do. Whether it's written in blood?" She shrugged. "Who knows."

Carlton laughed nervously. He felt better now they were talking but got the feeling she wasn't joking.

To hell with it! You can only die horribly in an abandoned building once.

He started to head down the rungs of the ladder.

Mabel stopped him.

"Hold on a second." She handed him the crowbar.

"Uh, what's this for? It's not gonna make it any easier to climb this ladder."

"You might need it. For, you know, stuff."

Not feeling better, Carlton took the crowbar and continued down the ladder. He had to concentrate on his footing until he reached the bottom, but when he had both feet on the ground, he looked around.

The basement smelled strange, but at first, he couldn't say why. The glowsticks provided enough light to see, although most of that was concentrated at the foot of the ladder. He was in a big workshop with benches and mounts for different tools scattered around. To get a better look, he'd need to spread the glowsticks out to provide more light.

He tossed a few of them around the basement, then picked up a bundle to use as a torch. With glowsticks in his hand, he looked at the tables, in search of Mabel's book.

There, over near the far wall. He was sure he spotted a ledger like the one Mabel was looking for. It was sitting on a bench with random things around it. He started advancing across the room but stopped when the glow-sticks revealed what seemed to be a leg on the wall.

He raised the glowstick bundle and followed the leg, which seemed to be part of a human body. As he did, he saw a dead man hanging from the wall in a thick set of metal chains. That wasn't the only body, either.

Bodies dangled from chains on the far wall. Others were lashed to the base of the same wall. Carlton was familiar with the dead, so they didn't hold any horror for him, but these were different.

For one thing, all were wizened and faintly smelled of embalming fluid. That was the strange smell permeating the basement. For another, the bodies all had pieces of metal, plastic, and glass riveted or sutured to or fused with their embalmed flesh.

When Carlton held up the glowsticks to reveal their faces, some of the bodies were wearing masks.

No, not masks, he realized, *but more weird alterations.*

They didn't look human. They looked like creatures from a B-rated horror films, but only if those creatures were real.

What kind of weirdo spends his time attaching fancy prosthetics to dead bodies?

Carlton stared in quiet horror, then strode over to the bench with the ledger on it. As he got closer, he got a better look at the bench. It was wide enough to be called a table and covered with tools. Some were bladed, others clawed, and many were hard to describe, with pieces that rotated or pushed in and out.

Amidst the tools, someone was piecing together another body. This one looked different, the work more precise than the others. The mechanical bits were more artful, almost beautiful, and covered with scrollwork and etching.

For some reason, this corpse was more special than the other crude examples hanging from the wall.

Had those been practice works for this final masterpiece? Who would think to create something like this, never mind devoting so much effort and attention to it?

Distracted by the masterpiece, Carlton delayed grabbing the ledger. It took a moment for him to remember and reach for it.

He wanted to get the hell out, no matter how weirdly compelling this mad creation was. It was as if he'd been distracted by a crazy piece of *avant garde* art and forgotten how horrifying it was.

As his hand touched the ledger, Carlton was distracted again. His eyes were drawn to those hanging things. He couldn't shake the feeling they were watching him. It made no sense since they were dead.

Yet, he couldn't shake the feeling.

When he held up the glowstick bundle, the light reflected from the eyes of the dead. At first that was all it was. Then suddenly, there was another light there, cold and hungry.

The dead were *watching* him. Every hair on his body stood on end, and then it got worse. Some of the dead things moved. They were struggling with their chains, straining to reach him!

SHIT!

CHAPTER THREE

Carlton recoiled and stumbled back, managing to get clear of the horrors. A handful of dead fingers flashed in front of him, reaching for the front of his shirt as he threw himself back.

Another hand swung at him, grasping hungrily. Sheer panic kept his feet blindly moving back until he lost his balance and fell on his ass.

At first, he thought he'd evaded them, but watching them from the basement floor, he saw the truth. Their arms were outstretched and grasping, but they couldn't quite reach him.

He could stand where he was all day long, and as long as he didn't take a step forward, the dead would not be able to touch him.

He later wondered why he hadn't screamed. It wasn't every day you got attacked by the living dead. It only seemed natural to cry out in horror, or at least in surprise. Instead, he'd stayed mute. Maybe he had been so shocked that he hadn't been able to scream and couldn't do anything but stumble away until he fell.

Carlton got his feet under him. Now that the initial shock was gone, he stared at them as they strained to reach him. They'd seemed real when they'd taken him by surprise, but now he thought they might not be as terrifying as he'd at first believed.

He wasn't going to call them zombies. He wasn't twelve years old, and whatever these things really were, they couldn't be living dead.

He picked up the crowbar from where he'd dropped it, looking at the chained monstrosities. He decided to take a swing, thinking this had to be a sick joke.

Yes. This was all part of whatever test Mabel had brought him here for.

It was in bad taste as far as he was concerned, but when he swung the hefty bar, he'd discover the truth. These were either going to turn out to be very convincing animatronics or highly skilled and creepily skinny actors.

They'd either break or bleed, and whichever happened, this little prank would be over. Whoever was running this scam wasn't going to want him smashing their stuff. Or their people, for that matter.

They'd be forced to own up to keep him from trashing everything, and if they *were* actors, they deserved to get a broken bone or two for what they'd put him through.

Carlton pulled the crowbar back, then swung at the legs dangling from the ceiling. He was angry and scared and he swung hard, so when the crowbar hit the leg, the bone snapped like a piece of kindling.

He had to admit that it looked convincing. It looked like

a corpse leg that had been hit hard by a crowbar. It didn't fall off, but part of the bone jutted out through the skin, sharp and jagged and horribly painful-looking.

It might have been painful, but the hanging thing didn't show it. It wasn't struggling any less than or any more than it had before. It was acting like the crowbar strike had been irrelevant.

Carlton felt a sinking sensation in the pit of his stomach, but it was too late to give up now. If he was going to start hitting dead people with crowbars, he'd better not stop until the job is done.

Deciding to try his luck, he pulled back to take a swing at one of the things hanging on the far wall. This time, the end of the crowbar managed to hook through one of the corpse's metal joints. The thing's arm broke off at the elbow and hit the floor.

Unfortunately, that didn't seem to demotivate the severed arm. It proceeded to claw, squirm, and drag itself across the floor toward him.

Son of a bitch!

He might not believe that was a severed arm, but he didn't want it anywhere near him. He stepped back as the awful thing crawled over and raised his crowbar to deliver a finishing strike.

When he smashed it into gooey pieces, he would reveal the prank for what it was. That was exactly what he tried to do, but it didn't work out the way he'd hoped.

He hit the thing once, but it was a glancing blow, and the arm didn't slow down. Aiming more carefully, he hit it again, but the thing kept dragging itself along by its fingers even though it was now a broken arm.

Carlton proceeded to pulverize the attacking limb, using the crowbar to reduce it to a semi-liquid slop no longer solid enough to pull itself along. No gears or circuits were revealed. Everything pointed to it being an honest-to-God animated corpse arm.

He looked at the hanging dead bodies in horror, all straining to reach him. They were trying even harder now, with the chains cutting through their dead flesh and grinding on their mechanical prosthetics. A few looked like they might break free of their chains.

As far as Carlton could tell, they could not be killed. He would have to reduce their bodies to mush to get them to stop attacking.

One of the bodies hanging from the ceiling was twisting and writhing more violently than the others as if the supernatural force animating it was stronger or more determined. It was twisting so violently against its chains and prosthetics that it seemed to be on the verge of tearing itself in two.

As Carlton stared at it in horror, the thing came apart. The bottom half of its body fell uselessly to the floor, where the legs kicked and flailed like they didn't know what to do with themselves.

The top half of the body dropped from its chains a moment later, hit the floor with a wet squelch, and started frantically scrabbling toward Carlton, its eyes desperate and hungry.

No way. Fuck this!

He bolted for the ladder. As the thing dragged itself toward him across the floor, he climbed the rungs, no thought in his head except to get away and keep running until the nightmares stopped.

A shadow fell across his face, and he heard Mabel's voice. "Oh, Carlton."

He looked up, his jaw dropping when he saw she'd dragged a large piece of machinery through the basement access. She was tipping it over the open trap door, blocking his escape route.

"Mabel, what are you doing? Stop fucking around!"

"I don't see my ledger, Carlton."

"Fuck your ledger! And fuck you! Have you seen the things down here?"

"I've seen more than you can imagine, Carlton, and I'm telling you this. One good hard shove on this thing, and it will come right down on your head. That would probably kill you, but you'd be lucky if it did. If you're not lucky, it will get wedged and trap you down there. I wouldn't wish that on my worst enemy."

Carlton hated her at that moment. "Why the fuck are you doing this to me?"

"Because I need to stop those things from getting out. That's my job. You might have noticed that they're...highly motivated."

"Highly motivated? You're fucking crazy! This thing just ripped itself in half, and it's *still* coming at me!"

"Yes, they're like that. So, you can either get that ledger so I can stop those things from coming after you, or I'm dropping this big hunk of metal down there to make sure they can't ever get out."

The half-corpse had now reached the bottom of the

ladder and was grabbing at Carlton's feet from below. One of its hands found a rung, and it started to pull itself up. Carlton kicked it in the face, then frantically swung the crowbar, trying to get it away from him.

"What happened to giving me a choice?" he screamed.

Mabel's voice was as cool as ever. "You do have a choice, Carlton. Complete the mission, or die."

Snarling in fury and fear, Carlton kicked at the half-corpse until it fell to the floor, then went down the ladder, swinging his crowbar until its skull caved in. When he turned to face the room again, he saw that some of the others had torn free, creating a gauntlet he would have to run to reach the ledger.

Carlton vaguely remembered an Iroquois custom where prisoners of war had to run the gauntlet between two rows of the tribe's warriors, being beaten and kicked the whole way. This wasn't like that, though. If he fell during this run, he wouldn't only be kicked or hit. He'd be ripped apart.

On the other hand, he *did* have a crowbar.

Wishing he hadn't pushed himself so hard in his workout but his muscles thrumming with adrenaline, he clenched his teeth. "Let's do this."

He moved forward swinging, hitting a dead thing so hard its brains slid out of the hole in its face. The thing stumbled and fell, knocking over another of the creatures.

He swung his crowbar again, breaking another creature's shoulder. His third swing knocked out a dead thing's eye. Harnessing the adrenaline pumping through his veins, Carlton focused on taking the monsters out of the fight by breaking limbs and crushing heads.

He used the crowbar and whatever else he could get his hands on, grabbing a tool when he reached the bench and plunging it into an open mouth and out the back of the monster's head. He hit another in the face and knocked out its teeth, which didn't stop it from gumming at him.

The horrors seemed to feel no pain. He wasn't sure they could die. On the other hand, they could be broken, and they weren't fast or strong. This was a good thing since the creatures outnumbered him, and as time went on, more freed themselves.

He had to get this done before they overwhelmed him. He snatched up the ledger and turned to fight his way back to the ladder.

He struck a downward blow, dropping a creature coming at him. He struck an upward blow, taking another one under the jaw and knocking it off its feet.

Carlton reached the ladder and started clambering up, hampered by the need to carry both the crowbar and the ledger. He needed the ledger to get out of there alive, but he didn't want to give up the crowbar. It was a weapon, and he didn't want to be without one.

The dead things followed him, some flopping and flailing up the ladder, others crawling up the walls like bugs, their senseless fingers finding purchase despite how badly it strained their flesh and bones.

Carlton got to the top, but Mabel didn't help him pull himself through the trapdoor. Instead, she waited with her piece of heavy machinery, then levered it through the opening after Carlton scrambled out of the way.

It crashed to the floor below, taking out a few of the

creatures on the way down. Unfortunately, it didn't seal up the access the way she'd hoped.

"Oh, dear. That's slowed them down, but it hasn't stopped them."

Carlton glanced through the trapdoor and saw the dead things were crawling over the piece of machinery to reach for the ladder.

Mabel frowned. "Do you have that ledger, Carlton? I think it's time we used it."

He stared at her with loathing and amazement. This woman had threatened to trap him down there with those creatures so she could get her hands on this weird *notebook?*

She turned to him. "The ledger. Now!"

He handed it over.

Mabel was clearly used to giving commands. "Keep any of them from getting up here so I can have a look at this."

Carlton went and stood over the trapdoor. A hand grabbed the edge, and he swung his crowbar so hard he broke every finger on it, sending the creature tumbling back to the floor below.

An arm reached up from the depths, and he saw the creature whose eye he had knocked out a few minutes earlier. The eyeball was dangling on the thing's dead cheek, and its mouth was gaping. He kicked it in the face until it lost its hold and fell.

Mabel was looking at the ledger. "Hmm," she muttered. "I'm sure this is the ol' Chaldean special, but there's only one way to know for sure, given the circumstances."

She produced a lighter with all manner of odd symbols

carved into it. When she lit the flame, it turned out to be a deep, rich red.

Carlton glanced nervously at her as he fought to keep the dead things from reaching the surface. He'd never seen a flame that color, and it didn't look natural.

Nothing about this situation was natural.

Mabel stared at the red flame. "This will either work really well or end very poorly."

Carlton beat down another undead arm that was reaching up to pull him in. "What?"

He swung the crowbar, and it hit the dead thing's head and got stuck in its un-zombie skull. Why "un-zombie?" Because zombies weren't real.

Carlton could not and would not allow himself to admit these were zombies. Not even if this one *was* trying to eat him alive.

"Just be ready to run," Mabel told him, her voice calm despite the circumstances.

Carlton fought to tear the crowbar out of the un-zombie's head while it tried to reach him with its teeth.

"What?"

Mabel held the red flame to the corner of the ledger. "Well, here goes nothing."

The red flames engulfed the ledger. Mabel smiled broadly, the most sincere-looking smile she'd produced since meeting Carlton. He was too busy to notice or see her watching the dead things crawling toward them smoke and smolder. They didn't seem to mind, but they were heating up fast.

Carlton backed away from the trapdoor, crowbar in hand, eyes fixed on the smoke pouring out of the creature with one eye. There was a sound like an oven lighting, and it was engulfed in red flames. Its mouth went on snapping at Carlton as the fire consumed its body.

Mabel's eyes went wide, but before she could do anything, the creature detonated like a bomb, sending corpse parts and metal shards flying in all directions. The eyeball that had been dangling on its cheek flew into the room and stuck to the ceiling, where it hung like it was watching what went on below.

Mabel's smile disappeared. This clearly had not been part of the plan.

She turned to Carlton with something like panic in her eyes. "DAMMIT! RUN!"

He stared at her for a second before he processed what was happening. She wasn't telling him to stay and fight anymore. She was telling him to run. If this woman thought he should run, he should run faster than he had ever run in his life.

She took off, and Carlton followed. They moved through the building while dead things exploded in the basement below them.

After a few desperate seconds, Mabel found the window they'd come in through. She flung herself through it, and Carlton dove out a half-second later.

As his body passed through the window, the building was rocked by an explosion of red flame, and shrapnel hurtled out of it. Arms, legs, and heads flew past them, along with pieces of broken-down machinery.

Carlton was so shaken that he stood still, not knowing whether he'd been hit by flying debris. Then the building caught fire, and they scrambled back from the heat.

A wall caved in, taking part of the roof with it. The building was collapsing, and with it, all evidence of the horrible things he'd seen inside.

Shaking off the shock, Carlton decided it was high time he got answers. He'd done what Mabel asked, but he had no intention of staying quiet. She needed to tell him the truth.

"Okay, Mabel. Start talking," he ordered grimly, but she wasn't easily intimidated.

"I've got answers for you, but you won't get them until you get in the car with me."

That set Carlton off. "Are you kidding? Listen, what's your deal? Did you grow up with servants or something? I'm not here to follow orders. What I saw in there was awful. I still don't know if I believe it, but *you* seemed to know your way around it, so I'll tell you what..."

He gripped the crowbar firmly and raised it an inch or two. Her eyes went to it, showing that she was well aware of the potential danger.

Carlton continued. "You either tell me what those things were down there, or I assume you're...I don't know, a *witch* or something."

"Thou shalt not suffer a witch to live, eh, Carlton?" She smiled her cool little smile, but she was not impressed. "I need you to think about this. We have a burning building here. Now, it's true that the authorities have done a good job of ignoring this part of the city, but they can't let this fire go on unchecked. So, we've only got a small window before emergency vehicles and a lot of curious people with phones start showing up. Do you really want to be hoofing it out of here when that happens?"

Carlton wasn't yet ready to give up on the intimidation. "Maybe I'll just take your car. Or maybe I'll rough you up first for trapping me in a basement with…with…"

He couldn't bring himself to say zombies out loud.

Mabel laughed. "Not very chivalrous, are you? Anyway, you don't know where I parked."

Carlton felt stupid, scrambling to get leverage on this woman who had nearly gotten him killed. "Maybe I'll wait until we get there, then I'll take your car. Or maybe I'll take my chances and run, and you'll never…"

"Never what? You're hardly indispensable."

Carlton looked at her. He knew when he was beaten. He couldn't force this woman to tell him a thing.

Mabel kept going. "Or maybe you give me your word that you won't try to kill me until after I give you an explanation, and we get the hell out of here."

Carlton was thinking hard, but his thoughts were interrupted by two things: a crash from inside the building and the distant sound of sirens. He winced.

"Okay, fine."

Mabel didn't move. "Your word, please."

"What, are we ten?"

Mabel raised her eyebrows and crossed her arms. "You heard me."

Carlton was flustered. If she was so concerned about emergency services, why wasn't she moving?

"Fine. You have my word."

She smiled again, this time without the hint of coldness her smiles generally held. Carlton suddenly had the impression this had been good fun as far as she was concerned.

"That's more like it," she told him. "Come on. I parked over here."

Who was this woman? What were those awful creatures? What had she gotten him into? If he wanted answers to those questions, Carlton had no choice. Shrugging in resignation, he followed her into the night.

CHAPTER FOUR

Mabel and Carlton got into her car, and she drove them well clear of the area and into the flow of traffic nearby before she said anything. They saw emergency vehicles going by to tame the blaze.

"Okay, start explaining," Carlton ordered, but as far as he could tell, Mabel didn't hear him.

A few minutes later, he tried again. This time, she held up a single finger to tell him to wait.

When he asked the third time, she finally answered him. "I will, Carlton, but first things first. We need to get you cleaned up. Then we can discuss everything over food."

Carlton frowned. "I'm not hungry."

She seemed amused. "I expect not, given that you're covered in corpse bits, embalming fluid, and ash."

For the first time, Carlton realized he was filthy. Beyond filthy, he was repulsive. The smell of embalming fluid and burned hair, the memory of everything that happened…

Those overwhelmed him, and he wanted to puke. Mabel knew this was coming, so she whipped the car out of traffic to make an abrupt stop. As the car jerked to a halt, Carlton managed to open the door and puke on the street.

When he was done, he closed the door, collapsed back into the seat, and looked at Mabel.

"You knew that was going to happen?"

Mabel nodded. "I have done this a time or two. On top of that, I don't want to have to drive around with your mess stinking up the car."

Carlton's head swam, but a thought occurred to him. "You've done all this before, and this is the best way you know to give a field test?"

Mabel chuckled. "You bet! What you just experienced was the fruit of years of professional development, all of it contributing to the creation of a singularly productive hiring experience. I mean, I thought it went well, didn't you?"

Carlton's jaw was hanging open. "You are insane."

Mabel sniffed with mock indignation. "Fine, be that way. Just be glad you weren't my first. Imagine how awful that one was."

"I'd rather not, thank you. I just got done being sick, and I'd like to put some distance between me and that experience."

Without another word, Mabel started driving. After a few minutes, Carlton started drumming his fingers on the dashboard. "Where are we headed?"

"Well, you've cleansed your palate now, so you're bound to be hungry in a little bit."

"Cleansed my pallet."

"Yes." She wove through traffic and pulled up in front of a restaurant called López Kitchen.

"What is this place?" he asked her.

"It's a Cuban diner. These guys serve immaculate Cuban cuisine."

"Cuban food? Huh."

He wouldn't have guessed Mabel would be into that, but it was big in Miami, so you never knew. "What do you recommend?"

"I'm not recommending anything. You go straight into the restroom and clean up, and I'll order us some food."

There she was, giving orders again. He didn't care, though, as long as he got some answers. He'd eat whatever she ordered for him, hear what she had to say, and decide whether it made sense.

Worst-case scenario, he'd get a free dinner out of it. It was the least she could do for him.

Having decided on a course of action, Carlton headed to the restroom. His plan was to clean up, but he slipped into wondering.

He was trying to figure out how things had changed so fast. This morning he had taken a big gamble by interviewing for the FBI. Now he was standing in the bathroom of a Cuban diner, having survived a battle with a horde of terrifying undead creatures.

As he stared at his face in the mirror, he realized that he was experiencing fear, disgust, curiosity, wonder, anger, resentment, and a wild optimism about the future that made no sense.

He wondered if he was having a mental breakdown.

Cycling through all these contradictory emotions at once was disorienting, making him feel like he must be losing it. He shrugged.

Mental breakdown or not, he looked like shit. The only thing he could do was clean himself up, and the only way to do so was to go through the motions. He foamed his hands with a lot of soap, then wiped off his face. He rinsed his hands and splashed water on his face, then ran his wet hands through his hair.

It wasn't perfect, but he was surprised to find he felt much better.

He started going through his mental process to make sense of things. This was a set of questions like the ones he asked when he was afraid, but they weren't the same.

Question one: What is my goal?

His goal was the same—Marly and Tully. Marly had told him that he had something to prove, and she didn't believe what she'd seen of him so far.

Question two: What do I need to achieve my goal?

He needed two things. He needed information, and he needed to keep living. In practical terms, that meant he needed to work with Mabel for the time being.

He had no other options for understanding what he'd seen, and based on what she had told him, he would have no other opportunities.

He understood what he needed to do. He looked at himself in the mirror and nodded at his reflection. "Resolved: if Mabel tells me what I need to know, I'll go on working with her."

"You do that, buddy." A man pushed past him on his

way out of the bathroom, and Carlton laughed. If this guy only knew.

As scrubbed as he could get and with his mind set on doing what he must, Carlton left the bathroom. Mabel was waiting for him. She'd been munching on crispy fried plantains as she waited, so it seemed like she'd expected him to be there for a while.

Carlton moved to sit across from her in the booth and was surprised to find the battered and stained crowbar waiting for him.

"What's this doing here?"

She smiled, amused. "I brought it in in case you decide you need to use it. I did promise you could try to kill me after I told you what was up."

"You think I'll need a crowbar?"

She nodded. "As strapping as you are, you'll need all the help you can get to kill me if that's what it comes down to."

Carlton wasn't sure what to make of this but decided to go along with it and sit down. No sooner was he in the booth than a server brought two plates, each of which contained a thick, flat sandwich.

"The Cubano," Mabel told him. "One of the greatest sandwiches in the world. Ham, roasted pork, Swiss cheese, pickles, and mustard, all smashed in a hot press."

With those words, Mabel dug in. Carlton was slower, but her assertion turned out to be right. All that fighting and puking had created a calorie deficit, and he needed to get some food into him.

Ham, Swiss cheese, pork, pickles, and mustard. From the first bite, Carlton was convinced that Mabel was right. The Cubano was one of the greatest sandwiches that had ever existed. He could feel himself getting better with every bite.

As he ate, Mabel talked. "I'm sorry for the rough introduction to the work I do, but it is a tradition in the organization that I represent. Truth be told, I don't approve of hazing, but at the same time, if I failed to give you a proper induction, you would struggle to bond and build rapport with the other operatives."

Carlton stared at her. "Uh-huh. So, trapping me in a basement with a bunch of…creatures was for my own good. Well, if that was a test, I ran away. Are you sure you want me?"

Mabel shrugged. "You did exceptionally well, even though you did try to chicken out. If you tell other operatives about that part, they will all lie and say they didn't have a similar moment in their inductions. Nobody likes to admit this stuff terrified them when they were introduced to it. To avoid that friction point, I'd suggest not telling anyone that I had to threaten to drop a few hundred pounds of rusted metal on your head to get you to finish the job."

"Noted," Carlton replied drily.

She smiled. "All right, then. Any questions so far?"

"Yes. Do you represent a covert branch of the FBI? One that deals with this...well, whatever this stuff is?"

"Yes…and no."

"Yes and no? What kind of answer is that?"

"Just keep eating your Cubano, Carlton. It will all be clear to you soon."

He looked at the half-eaten sandwich in his hands. It was threatening to fall apart. A long strand of roast pork hung from the back of the sandwich, dripping mustard on his plate.

It did seem like good advice. He lifted the sandwich above his face, gobbled the dangling shred of pork, and went back to eating the rest of the sandwich.

Mabel resumed talking. "Yes, we deal with paranormal, supernatural, and otherwise poorly defined anomalies. No, we don't work for the FBI or any other branch of the government. On the other hand, we have connections across multiple agencies. Otherwise, we would never have known to reach out to you."

As Mabel was saying, "paranormal, supernatural, and otherwise poorly defined anomalies," the waitress walked by with a Cuban latte and fried plantains. She heard those words, rolled her eyes, and shook her head. Carlton figured it was no big deal. You heard all kinds of crazy things, working a job like this.

"Why do all these agencies work with you if you aren't part of the United States government?"

"Because the government has had a policy in place for a long time. They work with our organization by finding special candidates for us."

"Special? Special how?" he asked, although he was sure he knew.

"Candidates they can't hire. People with potential, which can mean a lot of different things, but whom, for both ethical and legal reasons, they cannot employ. When they come across such a candidate, the government informs my organization."

"You're telling me they know about those things in the basement?"

Mabel chuckled. "Those things in the basement are just the tip of the iceberg. And no. Most of the government officials involved in this program have no idea what my organization does. That information is only available to the highest echelons. Most of them only know there's a program for otherwise unemployable candidates. They probably assume it's a black ops unit, which, in a sense, is true. Why tell them more than they need to know?"

I thought my cover was foolproof. Carlton wondered where his supplier had messed up. *Maybe these guys aren't fools.*

Carlton was done with his Cubano, so he sipped his lime soda and gazed at Mabel, trying to figure her out. He would have said she was crazy, except that he had seen those things with his own eyes. He had seen that they wouldn't die, not even when you ripped them into pieces or beat them into wet pulp.

It made sense. If those things were real, and so were other things equally weird, someone had to deal with them. Otherwise, they would have overrun the Earth by now.

The government wouldn't want to do it. Hell, the government wouldn't want to *admit* those things existed. If there was an organization that could do it for them, giving them much-needed plausible deniability…

Yeah, they would do that. He could believe that story. At least provisionally, he was willing to accept Mabel's account of who she worked for.

"Okay. What is the organization called, and what do they do? Besides scaring the shit out of former dark operatives, of course."

"Our full official name is the Society for Unexplained,

Unquiet Ephemera. I'll admit, that's a flowery name, and it doesn't explain anything. It was the name we were given on the organization's founding in the 1890s."

"In the 1890s? Don't you know the actual date?"

"We've had trouble maintaining and preserving our records. Particularly when it comes to our early years, we still don't know some things. Anyway, that's the full and original name. It usually gets abbreviated to the SUUE, but that's changed lately. The younger generation calls it the UUE, and they sometimes use other words with those same initials. In effect, we have several names."

"That makes you even more mysterious."

"I suppose it does. In any case, we have long operated as a private arm working in close contact with the government, helping them deal with supernatural threats and phenomena they can't acknowledge, much less deal with, without causing a mass public panic. That's why the government gives us access to candidates who are capable but otherwise untouchable—so they can engage in an ongoing series of operations to keep the inhuman forces of this world from doing too much damage or having undue influence on humanity."

"Sounds like a lonely job," he commented.

"I wouldn't say that. As you'll soon find out, the people you'll work with become a second family. I'll admit it's often a thankless job and frequently a dangerous one, as you've discovered. But it pays well, comes with a strong benefits package, including a great life insurance policy, and more than all that, this is a calling."

He raised his eyebrows. "A *calling*?"

"Yes." Her voice was firm. "This is bigger than politics

and private agendas, all that petty bullshit. The members of the UUE often joke with each other, saying the letters stand for Unwanted, Unknown, and Expendable, but the reality is that without our efforts, the world would be a very different place and not for the better. I truly believe there is no better job than this one."

Carlton dropped his gaze to the remainder of the Cubano on his plate. A few minutes ago, in the bathroom, he'd decided to work with Mabel as long as he could accept what she was about to tell him. Well, she'd told him. Could he accept it?

"Look, Carlton," Mabel continued. "I'll make no bones about it. I know that you have a checkered past. I know you have a lot of secrets. I also know you've found something worth trying to change your life for, and I'm happy to help you with that.

"It isn't working for the FBI, but that was never an option for you. If you work with me, you will still be helping people and protecting them from some really bad stuff. If you're willing to trust me and not use that crowbar on me, I can help you work toward getting something like a happily ever after."

What did she mean? How could she know he had a good reason to change his life? Did she know about Marly and Tully?

Carlton looked at her suspiciously, trying to figure out how much of what she was saying was the real deal and how much of it was manipulative recruiting bullshit. He tried to figure out how deep into his life she'd gotten and if it would be possible to escape from her clutches if he ever decided to.

Finally, he shrugged. "What do you need from me to make this happen?"

She smiled. "We always tell new recruits they need three things. I think the original phrasing was wordier, but that's the old SUUE for you. It went something like this: *The candidate for the Society for Unexplained, Unquiet Ephemera must not be grudging of the sweat of his brow nor of the substance in his veins. Most of all, he must be determined when he needs to be, and ruthless when his duties call for it.*"

Carlton looked at her. "Huh?"

"You've got to be willing to sweat, bleed, and kill. That's what it means, and it's what we ask of every UUE operative. You're already good at all three, aren't you?"

Carlton looked her in the eyes. "That's right. I am."

"So, what's your decision, Carlton? Does the UUE have a new recruit, or do we need to see how good you are with that crowbar?"

She would not have left the crowbar in the booth if she wasn't confident that she could handle whatever he tried to do with it. Still, there was no reason to let her get overconfident.

He looked her in the eyes, and she didn't look away. Her eyes didn't leave his as he stretched one hand to rest on the crowbar, smiling coldly.

Why was he doing this? When he thought about it later, he wasn't sure. Maybe he was sick of her high-handed ways and wanted to show her that she couldn't push him around.

Maybe he wanted her to see he was not afraid to use violence since that's why she was hiring him.

Maybe he wanted to assert power in a situation that had made him feel powerless.

For a second, he saw something that might be fear on her face. It was gone so fast he wasn't sure, but they both knew he wasn't going to hit her with the crowbar.

His mind was made up, and there was only one course of action. He pulled his hand back.

"All right. I'll work with you. I'll work with the UUE. But first things first. Are you going to finish that Cubano?"

She looked at her plate, where the second half of her sandwich sat untouched. "I usually can't eat a whole one. You go ahead. Otherwise, it will end up in my fridge, and I don't know when I'll get home again."

He took the rest of the Cubano off her plate and wolfed it down, marveling at his appetite. Whatever else you could say about fighting the dead, it helped you appreciate a good sandwich. He washed it down with the rest of the bright green lime drink, then looked at Mabel again.

"Okay. What's the plan?"

She got up with a smile. "Come along, and bring the crowbar with you. You never know when one of those might come in handy."

As they walked out the door into the Miami night, Carlton was taking a step into a new world, one he hadn't known about. The question was, would he survive it, or was this going to turn out to be the last in a long line of bad decisions?

CHAPTER FIVE

When Mabel pulled up in front of a small chapel and parked, Carlton thought he had it figured out.

"Uh-huh. I should have seen it coming."

Mabel glanced at him, much as you would look at a man who had just said something stupid. "Should have seen what coming?"

He shrugged. "I'm just saying. I should have expected it."

"You're going to have to expand on that." Her voice had a hint of impatience, like this wasn't the first time she'd had this conversation.

He gestured vaguely. "That you guys are working with the Catholic Church. I mean, it figures. What's the only thing nearly as big as the government?"

Mabel shook her head, though he couldn't tell whether she was irritated or amused. "We don't work for the church, Carlton. Sorry to confuse you. We do sometimes work alongside members of various faith groups, as we work with the government to a certain extent. We don't work with the church as often as you might think since we often have different objectives."

Carlton frowned. "Different objectives? What do you mean?"

"Well, depending on who you are dealing with, you can get one of those dewy-eyed types on a mission to save some creep's soul."

"Uh-huh. Whereas our objective..."

"Is to put the son of a bitch down before they hurt people."

Carlton nodded. "I see."

Mabel continued. "If you want to save souls, you can retire your dick and join a monastery. While you're working for me, the priority is putting a stop to threats, not reforming the world's monsters."

"Makes sense to me, boss. I was wrong, but that doesn't explain what we're doing here. Is something about to pop up out of the graveyard?"

"Do you see a graveyard?"

He looked out the window. "No, I don't."

"If you want to understand what's going on, keep your eyes and ears open, and you'll pick it up. That's your first lesson as a new recruit. You don't *have* to ask questions. If I think you need to know something *now*, I'll explain it to you. Got it?"

"Yeah. I got it."

She nodded curtly. "Good."

She got out of the car, and Carlton followed her, perplexed. She still hadn't told him what they were doing at the church. Maybe that wasn't on the list of things he needed to know right now. Or, maybe he needed to do what she'd said and pay attention, and it would all be obvious soon.

She moved to the left side of the chapel with Carlton behind her and came to an exterior staircase that led down to a basement door. As they followed the staircase, Mabel started talking.

"I've got dirt on the priest who runs this chapel. He's naturally grateful that I haven't exposed him, so we're able to use the basement of the chapel as a safe house with a high degree of confidence. Privacy is important to us, as I'm sure you can understand."

"Sure. Of course I understand, but...dirt?"

He didn't want to think about the potential consequences of not exposing a priest if you had information on him.

"Not that kind of dirt," she clarified. "Like I told you, I'm not a monster."

Mabel entered a number on a keypad on the door, and they entered the basement of the little chapel. Inside, it was almost homey. It had plenty of cozy seating, a place for people to gather around a table for a meal, and a kitchenette to prepare said meal.

The only thing which might suggest that this was anything other than a friendly middle-aged aunt's apartment was the presence of two sets of military-style bunks in one corner, and the arms locker with crates of ammunition in the other.

There was also a space where the cinderblock wall had been broken into, exposing the dark earth like an open wound. A little shrine had been set up inside this alcove, although Carlton didn't get a close look at the shrine itself.

"Nice place," he commented. "A little spooky in parts, but…"

"Spooky?" She looked around. "I would have said it was downright welcoming."

"Sure. It's totally welcoming. If you don't count, you know, the weird shrine in the dirt. Or the weapons and ammunition."

"Oh yeah. That. Well, we do the best we can with what we've got. This is one of the nicest safehouses we have, honestly. Unfortunately, we're not going to be staying here for all that long."

"Why's that?" he asked her.

"Because you haven't been assigned a territory yet. We need a safe place to rest tonight before we head to the UUE headquarters for a full onboarding with the organization."

That made sense. The FBI had Quantico, and the CIA had the Sherman Kent School for Intelligence Analysis. It stood to reason that the UUE would have its own training facility.

Mabel continued. "For the moment, you're considered a candidate, or a supplicant, to use the fancy term."

"Supplicant? That sounds like the Masons."

"Well, that's what it originally was—a late nineteenth-century secret society, complete with supplicants and neophytes and so on. Our terminology has drifted over time, but we do sometimes use the original words."

"Okay," he replied, sitting down in one of the comfortable chairs. If they weren't going to be here for long, he might as well enjoy whatever comforts this place had to offer. "So, I'm a supplicant. As opposed to what?"

"An operative or a neophyte. I'll explain. If you do a

good job for the UUE, and if you survive long enough, you'll become an initiate of the Society, or, as we more often call it these days, an agent. If that should occur, you'll be given responsibility for your own area. That will mean it's your job to watch it and to oversee everyone who works for the UUE inside that area."

"Like a CIA station chief."

"Roughly equivalent, yes. You might even request to have your watch posted in the Northwest in the next few years."

It looked like she knew something about his intentions for Marly and Tully. He had no idea how she would since he had never told anyone. One thing he was learning about the UUE was that they were as well informed about their potential recruits as any intelligence agency he'd ever heard of.

It was shocking, but he shook it off. "Okay, you said we're staying the night? Does that mean we're leaving tomorrow morning?"

"There are a few things I have to clear up first before we can go, but as soon as those things are dealt with, yes. I'll take you to UUE headquarters for your onboarding, after which you'll begin your training."

This made him anxious. "But how can I leave? I mean, that isn't possible."

"Why not? You have to be ready to embrace change, Carlton."

"But all my stuff is still at my apartment, and there's the apartment itself. I can't break the lease. They'd charge me for all the remaining months, and it would make it almost impossible to get another apartment in the future."

He was flailing to delay the inevitable. This was all happening far too fast.

Mabel nodded at one of the bunks, where he saw a single box. "You know, it was almost sad how little you had in your apartment. And not to worry about the apartment, for that matter. The Society took care of the fees for leaving before your lease was up and paid the landlord enough to guarantee a good reference if you should ever need it."

Anger flashed through him like a lightning bolt. They hadn't even waited for his answer. They were so confident that he would do what they asked him that they had cleared out his apartment and moved the contents to this safe house.

Not that there was much in the way of contents. Mabel was right. When he saw the single box that held his earthly possessions, Carlton realized his life had been pathetic. Maybe with this new career with the UUE, he'd have the chance to build a real life.

There was more than that, too. "You know, Mabel, you must have been sure that I would survive my initiation, my hazing, or whatever you want to call it. And you must have been sure that I would choose to join up."

She shrugged. "I'm good at my job. We do a complete analysis before we approach a recruit."

"Psychological?"

"Psychological, financial, and everything. We need to know their motivations, their life circumstances, and their character traits. If you know all that, you generally know enough to predict a person's decisions."

"That might be so, but you've got no business making the decision for me."

"I'm surprised you're angry. When you were recruited by the CIA, did they respect your personal autonomy any better than I have?"

He shook his head. "No. Not really."

"Is this going to be a problem?"

He shook his head again. "I don't like the way you handled this, but it doesn't change my decision."

"Good. Is there anything else you need to know?"

"Why do we even need a safe house? I mean, the name implies somewhere safe to hide out. Are we in danger?"

"Let me ask you this," Mabel replied. "Did you think that ledger was written by one of those revenants chained up in the basement?"

"I haven't had much time to think about it, but no. If I'd been asked, I would not have guessed that the ledger was written by a brainless, man-eating dead man. Then again, it's been a weird day. I can't say for sure."

She laughed. "You've got a flexible mindset; I'll give you that. It's one of the best assets you could have in this line of work."

He shrugged. "I adapt to what's in front of me. I've been doing it for a long time."

"Yes. I know you have. Fair enough. If you'd had a chance to think about it, you would not have guessed that the ledger was written by the revenants."

"Revenants? That's what you call them?"

"Revenants, yes. The walking dead, or more accurately, the wrathful and dangerous walking dead. Why, what do you call them? Don't tell me you call them zombies."

"I wouldn't think of it."

"Glad to hear it. But no, the ledger and the revenants are both the work of a necromancer."

"A…necromancer? Where have I heard that word before?"

"I don't know, maybe Dungeons and Dragons? Maybe J.R.R. Tolkien? Or maybe you used to listen to Scandinavian black metal?"

He just shrugged.

Mabel continued. "A necromancer is a type of sorcerer who works with the dead. Traditionally this was mostly for divination, but these days, you never know. The necromancer can use the dead for any work he wants done. Anyway, that's only one of the many different kinds of creeps."

"Creeps?" he asked. "What's a creep?"

"That's Society slang. A creep is anyone supernatural or supernatural-adjacent. You'll be dealing with a lot of different creeps in your work for the Society."

"Necromancers, revenants. Okay. Jesus, what a world we live in. So, we're staying here in the safe house to protect us from the necromancer?"

From the look on her face, she didn't like the sound of that. "That makes it sound like we're running scared, which isn't the case. The Society knows how to handle creeps. It's not like we're constantly hiding from them."

"Then what's the deal, Mabel? Is that necromancer unusually dangerous? You said we needed a safe place to rest tonight. What do we need to be safe from?"

"Well, it's not that this necromancer is supremely skilled or careful, as far as I can tell. They left their grimoire lying around for us to grab. The ledger, I mean. Still, the sheer number of revenants they created is concerning. It shows that they're resourceful, for one thing. Sourcing dead bodies is not easy. It also shows they're aggressive, so there is a decent chance they'll be out for revenge. That's why we need a safe house. A necromancer's idea of revenge is often…twisted."

"Hmmm." He got out of the chair, went to the kitchen, and poured a glass of water. "I agree. It's best to keep your head down if someone is gunning for you."

"Oh, I wouldn't give it a second thought if someone was gunning for us. We'd shoot them first. This situation has the potential to get a lot worse than that."

"Worse than someone trying to kill us? What does that even mean?"

"It comes down to the nature of necromancy. A necromancer controls the dead and uses their bodies without permission. By definition, the necromancer has no respect for the rights of others."

He nodded. "Sure, I can see that. And?"

"Well, there are different types of monsters. Vampires, for instance. A vampire might be a bloodsucking corpse demon that will drain you dry, but usually, they don't bother to turn you. You'll get killed. A wraith might suck your life out through your breath, but when your life's gone, it's just gone. Skinchangers will rip you limb from limb after they eat your face off. That's an uncomfortable way to go, but in the end, all those things are only going to kill you. A necromancer though..."

She shuddered.

Carlton interrupted. "Hold on a minute. Vampires?

Wraiths? Skinchangers? You're telling me all those things are real? I'm going to be dealing with all of them?"

Mabel ignored him. "A necromancer can bind your soul to your body so it can't move on after death. Even when you're dead, you can't escape whatever horrible and humiliating things the necromancer does to people, especially those who cross him. Some necromancers get really creative about the awful things they'll do, so it's better for us if we don't let that happen."

None of that sounded good, but Carlton was still stuck on the idea of vampires.

"Mabel, listen to me. Vampires are real?"

"Yes." She shrugged. "Yes, vampires are real. I mean, a lot of things are real. Probably most of the things you've heard of and a fair number of things you haven't."

"Chupacabras?"

"Real."

"Huh." He remembered seeing a TV show that said chupacabras were based on a horror movie some woman saw, but if Mabel said they were real, then they were. That didn't answer his questions about vampires, though. "Hold on a sec. Don't vampires turn people into more vampires?"

"Those are the sorts of questions that will be answered during your training up north. For now, the most important thing is for you to get some sleep."

As soon as he heard those words, Carlton realized he was exhausted. That wasn't surprising, considering how much of the night he'd spent fighting revenants hand-to-hand with a crowbar.

The exhaustion hit him so suddenly that he knew it was the inevitable crash from the adrenaline and stress he'd been through that night. He'd regularly faced it throughout his life, so it was not a new or surprising feeling. Still, his head was full of more questions than he'd ever had before, and he wasn't sure he could rest. He could lie down, though, even if he wasn't sure he could fall asleep.

Carlton mumbled "goodnight" to Mabel, then went over to the bunk with his stuff on it. Looking down at his meaningless odds and ends, he couldn't help but agree with her that it was pathetic how few personal effects he had. How had his life brought him to this place with nothing to his name except these few useless items?

He put the box on the floor beside his bunk, exhausted physically and emotionally. Those were mixed with shame for his life and a powerful sense of optimism about the future. He felt like he was making the right choice. This was the road for him, wherever it led.

Besides, he liked owning only a few things. It felt self-disciplined and self-sufficient.

Habit kicked in, and he settled on the bed to rest, knowing his body would take over.

Before he dozed off, he saw Mabel head to the alcove in the exposed earth. She took out the strange lighter and placed it in the alcove, along with what looked like a pocketknife and a watch or bracelet.

He noticed for the first time that there was a grotesque and primitive-looking figure in the alcove. He couldn't see its features clearly, but there was an eerie and expressionless quality to it. Mabel touched it after laying her items down, then muttered something too low for him to hear.

As his eyes got heavy, Carlton wondered if he was hearing a low humming noise or if that was only his imagination. If it was there, it was in the background, like a song playing quietly in a neighbor's apartment. He didn't think it was a song.

He also wondered if he would have nightmares. That seemed reasonable after a night like the one he had experienced, but he was far from eager to see those gaping mouths and squirming body parts again.

His mind had barely formed the thought when his eyes closed and he fell into a deep sleep free of dreams. When he woke up, it seemed like he had been asleep for only a second.

There was a pounding on the door. He opened his eyes, realizing the sound must have woken him up. Mabel was moving toward the door with a pistol in her hand. Carlton didn't know where she had gotten the weapon.

"Who is it?" Mabel called. "I'm armed."

"Goddammit," a woman's harsh voice answered from outside. "You know who this is. Now open the door and let me in. *Please!*"

Her tone of voice was a mixture of aggression and desperation. Carlton couldn't decide whether the woman was demanding or begging.

"How do I know you're not being coerced?" asked Mabel.

"Let me in, or I swear to God…"

It wasn't a threat since she didn't finish the sentence. Whatever she meant to do if Mabel didn't let her in, she wasn't willing to spell it out.

It had an effect on Mabel, though. She put her ear up to the door and listened for a second, then glanced at Carlton, who was just getting up. Then she muttered a curse he couldn't hear as she opened the door.

In tumbled two women, supporting a much larger man between them. They lurched through the door and then sprawled on the floor as the big man's legs gave way.

One of the two was a tough-looking, whip-thin woman with ash-blonde hair. In the harsh voice with which she'd shouted through the door, she shouted, "Close the door! They're coming!"

CHAPTER SIX

There was no time for introductions. There was no time for Mabel to explain why she hadn't wanted to open the door. She started doling out instructions. Turning to the second woman through the door, she commanded, "Go, get the med kit."

The woman was short and compact and muscular. She was supporting the big man on the floor. When Carlton saw him, his first thought was, *That's a lot of blood! Is all that his?*

The woman jumped up at Mabel's order. When she left to get the med kit, Mabel whirled to face the thin blonde woman. "Jamie, secure the area."

Carlton was next. "Go get some hardware."

Carlton didn't jump like the others. He was too busy staring as Jamie drew a knife, sliced open her palm, and started smearing symbols on the door. He felt pressure in his ears and behind his eyes as the sigils took shape.

What the hell?

"Carlton!" Mabel snapped. "Get a move on!"

When he started moving, Carlton saw that someone had stripped the big guy's shirt off. The man's torso was covered with bloody bitemarks as if someone human or almost human had taken bites out of him like an apple.

Shuddering at the sight but eager to have some firepower in his hands, Carlton made a beeline for the arms locker. Throwing it open, he found several spots for firearms and other weapons: swords, axes, maybe a mace, but the locker was almost empty.

The only remaining weapons were a pair of pistols, bog-standard 9mm Rugers, and a bolt-action rifle more suited for deer hunting than urban combat.

He didn't understand the purpose of stocking a modern armory with medieval weapons, but those weapons must have seen use, or they would still be hanging here.

That's one of the many things they'll explain to me in training, assuming I live long enough to go through training.

Carlton heard everyone working frantically, and he didn't want to start out by being a slow and awkward rookie. He snatched up the weapons, then yanked open the crates on the floor to look for ammunition.

Inside one, he was grateful to find pre-loaded pistol magazines, along with a box of ammunition for the rifle. Carlton grabbed some and turned to scuttle back but paused to consider his limited options before snatching up the crowbar.

He made it to Mabel and saw she was working feverishly to stem the bleeding from the big guy's bites. Unfortunately, the big guy, whose name was apparently Mikey, also had a large hematoma on the side of his head.

That was indicative of a head injury, which explained

why he wasn't screaming. That, or he was too drained to. Either way, Carlton didn't like Mikey's odds.

With no time for introductions, Carlton was learning by listening. He'd heard Mabel address Jamie and Mikey, then learned the blonde's name was Amber.

Amber assisted Mabel until Carlton walked across the room, chambering a round in the rifle. Her face turned dark, and she clenched her jaw.

"Goddammit!" she exclaimed, "Where are the real guns?"

Carlton stammered an explanation, but Amber turned away in disgust and headed for the arms locker as if he were full of shit. He didn't appreciate the assumption, but she'd discover the truth for herself.

She came back looking morose but didn't apologize. Carlton got the impression that she didn't do that very often.

Looking frustrated, Jamie wrapped a kitchen rag around the hand she'd sliced open, then snatched a pistol. Carlton glimpsed the wound as she was wrapping it. It was a shallow slice, but not so shallow that it wouldn't scar.

If bloodshed was a necessity for raising magical power, it was clear to Carlton that anyone who did so would get covered in fine white lines.

"We're secure in front," Jamie reported, "But given what we were facing, there's a good chance they'll claw their way through the ceiling before too long."

"What's going on out there?" Mabel demanded.

Taking the other pistol from Carlton but leaving him the crowbar, Jamie angrily began her account. "I don't fucking know! It was supposed to be a straightforward goddamn surveillance mission. Real low impact, according to you. I don't know how the fuck you got your intel so wrong, but I'll tell you what, Mabel. I don't fucking appreciate it!"

Mabel gazed at her coldly. "I asked you what was going on, not how you felt about it."

"I'm fucking telling you. We got sent out on this fucking surveillance mission, supposedly low-risk, so we didn't even arm up. Our assumption, which turned out to be incorrect, was that any problems could be handled by Mikey's huge fists. Well, lo and behold, this little nothing surveillance mission turns into the biggest goddamn ambush I've ever seen!"

"Who or what ambushed you?" Mabel asked unsympathetically.

"It was a fresh-evant. As we were withdrawing from the surveillance location, I got tackled by a fresh-evant."

Carlton frowned. "What's a fresh-evant?"

Jamie threw him an impatient glance. "Who the hell's this guy?"

Mabel's voice was somewhat patient. "You know very well I was meeting a new recruit tonight. This is Carlton Priez Pierce. Carlton, fresh-evant is Society slang for a fresh revenant. They're typically faster and angrier than a revenant that's been dead for a while. Now hold off on the questions, so I can find out what happened."

Jamie went back to ignoring him and kept talking. "The fresh-evant tackles me, and Mikey hauls it off and curb-stomps it after an impressive choke slam, but that wasn't the only one. There were a dozen of these things, some so fresh their blood hadn't even dried, and we're talking some grisly executions here. We were overwhelmed. An unarmed surveillance mission and we were blindsided."

"That's why it's never a good idea to go unarmed," Mabel pointed out. "Yes, I said it should be low intensity, but that's only a guess. You don't trust your life to a guess."

Jamie glared at her, not appreciating the criticism after what she'd been through. She got it together and kept telling her story.

"We managed to fight our way to our vehicle, but Mikey took the worst of it, and we only barely managed to pull him in as we took off. The fresh-evants gave chase, but we floored it and outdistanced them. We knew we needed to get Mikey help in a secure place, so we brought him here."

"Okay." Mabel nodded. "We're almost caught up, but why did you say, 'They're coming?'"

"As we started to move Mikey out of the vehicle, I spotted some of the fresh-evants rounding the corner. They were searching the street."

Amber stepped into the conversation. "Is there a necromancer in Miami bold enough to pull a Romero? In the whole world? That shit hasn't happened in a long time."

Mabel turned to Carlton. "When a necromancer pulls a Romero, it means they have their creations move about openly. As Amber said, nothing like that has happened in a very long time."

Mabel held his gaze, and Carlton knew what she was thinking. This situation was their fault. By destroying the grimoire and a basement full of revenants, they had stirred up a necromancer.

She didn't say anything to the others about it. She finished bandaging Mikey, who was still out of it.

"Carlton, keep that hunting rifle in your hand. Don't put it down for any reason," she ordered, then pulled out her phone.

Before she could dial, they heard movement from above.

Carlton's eyes went to the ceiling, where a lot of scraping and bumping were accompanied by a quavering voice raised in protest.

Mabel cursed and rushed to the bunks, then to the wall behind them. She pressed on a section of cinderblock, which produced a puff of dust before turning to reveal a closet-sized space and a ladder leading up.

Jamie and Amber hissed in surprise and demanded to know what she was doing. From above came crashing and the sounds of things being ripped apart.

"Sounds like carpet," Carlton commented, but nobody seemed interested in his opinion. Something up there was furiously beating a hard surface, maybe tile, as Mabel rapidly climbed the ladder.

Shortly after she'd disappeared, they heard a pistol fire, then fire again. Jamie and Amber went to the ladder, with Carlton not far behind. A round-bellied man with thinning hair scrambled down the ladder, dressed in priest's vestments.

"Jesus!" Amber blurted, unintentionally blaspheming. "You surprised me, *Padre*. I almost attacked you."

A second later, Mabel joined them, then levered the hidden door shut. Within the wall, something clicked. The priest looked banged up, but it seemed the fresh-evants were not interested in him. Their only goal was to tear up the floor to get to those beneath. "I drew their attention with a few shots," Mabel explained. "That gave the padre a chance to make for the ladder."

Jamie wasn't impressed. She folded her arms and looked angrily from Carlton to the priest and back. "Uh-huh. Well, this is great. Just *great*."

"What?" Carlton asked her.

"This adds to our problems. We now have two hangers-on to take care of."

Carlton didn't like being called a hanger-on. "I'm not an amateur," he protested, but Jamie shot him down.

"Save it, new guy. You're not even a neophyte, which means that you don't know your ass from a hole in the ground. And no, I don't care what you did before Mabel scooped you up."

Mabel stepped in before things could get any more heated. "Shut up and listen, all of you. We're going to get out of here, and we're going to do it pronto. Our only chance is to work together, so if you two want to have a big old-fashioned drama with each other, it will have to wait until we get somewhere safe. You understand me?"

Jamie snarled but nodded.

Carlton nodded too. "All right by me."

"Good." Mabel's authority was beyond question, no matter how irritated the others were with her. "Listen to me, and there's a chance we'll all survive. This is how we're going to do it. Carlton and Amber are on Mikey-moving duty. Jamie will get the priest moving, and I'll cover you until you reach the church van in the parking lot across the street. We'll use that to make our escape. Everyone got it?"

The priest was shaking his head. "I'm sorry, but I-I don't have the keys!"

Mabel reached into the kitchenette drawer and produced a set of keys, grinning sardonically. "I might have made copies."

The priest was horrified. "So, it was *your* underwear I found in the back seat!"

Mabel shrugged. "Of course it was."

She didn't care how shocked Carlton looked. "I had to change clothes between operations, and I must have left them behind. And Padre, I'll note that you never tried to throw the underwear out or give them back."

The priest looked apoplectic, but Mabel shook her head and declared, "Pervert" before going back to reviewing the plan. Whatever Mabel had on this priest, it was heavy. He didn't even dare question her when she was insulting him.

From above, they heard clawing and scrabbling.

Amber looked up. "The way things are moving up there, it won't be long before they're coming through the ceiling."

Jamie nodded. "We need to find the necromancer and kill them. Whoever they are!"

Mabel was not convinced. "Have you seen them?"

"No, I haven't."

"Then the best thing we can do is regroup and come at this another way. We can't go for the win when our arms locker is empty and we've got civilians on hand."

When she said the bit about the arms locker being plundered, she looked angrily at the priest. He didn't say anything in response, just tried to sink through the floor.

"All right," Mabel told them. "Let's get moving."

Carlton used the shoulder strap to sling the rifle across

his back, slid the crowbar through his belt, then leaned over to help Amber heft Mikey. Mikey was a big guy, so it wasn't easy, but Carlton was shocked by how strong Amber was.

Given the different people he'd killed and the ways he had killed them, Carlton was keenly aware of the strength differential between men and women. He could tell from having Amber on the other end that she was easily as strong as he was and possibly stronger.

It was hard for him to imagine, never mind understand. She was smaller than him, for one thing, and for another, she was a woman. While he had met plenty of women who were stronger than the average man, it seemed incredible that someone so small could be that much stronger.

As they got Mikey up, Carlton pondered what a strange twenty-four hours it had been. His concept of reality had been tossed out the window, and the woman who had done the tossing had offered him a job.

Now he was helping a small woman carry a large man out of a Catholic chapel in which they were being besieged by the walking dead and pursued by a vengeful necromancer.

When he considered all that, it wasn't as strange to find that Amber was very strong. Still, he wished the new reality would slow down enough for him to catch up with it.

As the rest of them got ready to run, Mabel went to the shrine in the dirt alcove, muttered something, and extracted the items she had left there. Then, to Carlton's surprise, she picked up the idol and slammed it down sharply, breaking it.

Once the idol was in pieces, Mabel took a vial from the shattered clay. She didn't say a word, merely pocketed the vial, then returned to the rest of them. Whatever ritual she had performed, it went unexplained.

"Everybody ready?"

Amber replied sarcastically, "Ready to get overrun by angry corpses? Sure. One hundred percent ready."

Ignoring the sarcasm, Mabel turned to Carlton. "If you have to use that gun, either the heart or the head will work for this type of revenant. I mean the heart, though, not just the chest. Center mass won't cut it."

Carlton nodded. "Got it."

Standard training was to aim for center of mass since that takes out most opponents quickly and reliably while being much easier to hit than the head. If it came down to head or heart, though, head was the easier target.

Once everyone had confirmed they were ready to go for it, they burst through the door. Mabel led the way, pistol barking, and she was a damn good shot. As they ran behind her, they had to be careful to step over the collapsed revenants she'd left behind.

They made it halfway across the street before the chapel's doors burst open and a pack of fresh-evants rushed after them.

Newly dead as they were, the fresh-evants weren't decayed, but the soulless hunger in their eyes was more than enough to get Carlton moving. They ran with long, loping steps, impervious to pain or exhaustion. As he hobbled along with Mikey, trying to escape, Carlton knew they would keep going if he ran all day.

He heard chanting from somewhere nearby. The words

were indistinct, but the power behind them was sinister. Carlton glanced around and saw that the revenants Mabel had shot were getting back up.

He'd been in the shit so many times that he used to think he could no longer feel fear when his life was in danger. He knew better now. When the fresh-evants ran after him, Carlton felt fear like he had never felt before.

Jamie, beside him and a little behind, shouted, "The necromancer is here! Do you hear that chanting? We need to find that creep and kill his ass! Come on, Mabel! Let's end this!"

Mabel threw open the van door to let Amber and Carlton load Mikey.

"No!" she shouted. "Just stick to the plan!"

Jamie wasn't having it. "I see him! He's over there!"

Carlton caught a glimpse of the necromancer standing on a corner, a dark figure in a pale hooded sweatshirt. Jamie took off toward it, shooting any undead in her way. As she went after it, the figure retreated. Carlton unslung his rifle from his shoulder, intending to help her.

Mabel shouted, "Help the priest! They're about to get him!"

When he looked, Carlton saw that the priest was about to be swarmed by revenants. *Shit. Jamie will have to fend for herself.*

He dropped the leading one with a shot from his rifle, and it collapsed in front of the priest. As it did, Carlton's fighting instincts took over, and he ran in, smashing a dead thing's head with the buttstock.

It occurred to him the crowbar would be easier to swing, so he slung the rifle on his back again and pulled the crowbar out. He laid around him as he shoved the terrified priest into the van. The man looked like he was about to have a heart attack, but he did what Carlton wanted without complaint.

When Mabel started the van, Carlton saw that Jamie was surrounded, and the revenants were dragging her down. The thin woman was fighting desperately with what he assumed was hysterical strength, and she was hitting hard enough to send fresh-evants twice her size sprawling.

It wasn't enough. As Carlton watched, Jamie disappeared under the pack, screaming. Carlton looked at Amber and Mabel, thinking they might say something or show grief, but they only shook their heads, their eyes sad and grim.

As the van rolled out of the parking space and onto the road, one last revenant threw itself in front of them, slavering, its eyes empty yet hungry. They didn't slow down, just let the van flatten the awful thing.

CHAPTER SEVEN

The sun was finally coming up, and the horizon was that shade of luminous gray it turned seconds before bursting into color. It was morning, and they had survived the night. Well, some of them had.

Mabel drove through the streets of Miami, putting time and space between them and the necromancer's pack.

The priest had been muttering prayers since they'd left the chapel, although Carlton couldn't hear a word the man was saying. For all he knew, the prayers were in Latin.

Amber kept checking her phone for traffic updates so nothing would force them to stop. If they did, they might come under attack.

She also checked what the police were up to. "Looks like they responded to a disturbance. Location matches our chapel. They aren't reporting a riot or anything like that."

"What *are* they reporting?" asked Mabel.

"Just a public disturbance. That's it."

Carlton would have expected Amber to be upset or concerned about what she saw on the police reports, but she relayed the information as flatly as she had repeated the traffic reports.

Carlton supposed Amber's background was like his. She might be a former spook, although he didn't know which agency. That would explain it, but it was still chilling to watch somebody else be calm and professional about death and mayhem. Was that the impression he gave other people?

Carlton was still learning his way around Miami. He wasn't familiar enough with the city to guess their destination, but he got the impression that they weren't driving at random. Mabel seemed to be drifting in a consistent direction while doing her best to evade pursuit.

"Where are we going?" he asked.

"At the moment," replied Mabel, "we're headed to a safe place to drop off the priest."

"And after that?"

"After that, we are going to sort some stuff out. Hang in there, Carlton. You're a new recruit, but trust me when I tell you your first workday was not supposed to be like this."

So far, his first workday felt like his job interview, but Carlton kept that thought to himself. At least this time, he wasn't trapped in a basement. He felt better about fighting them when he could run if he had to.

"What happened out there?" Amber asked Mabel. "What set this off?"

Mabel set her jaw but didn't answer. As far as Carlton could tell, their successful raid on the necromancer's hideout had set off this catastrophe. Now Jamie was dead, and she had died ugly. It didn't surprise him if Mabel wasn't ready to talk about that.

They were nearly on the opposite side of the city from where they started when Mabel pulled the church van into the parking lot of a non-denominational mission and thrift store. The sign out front read, Holy Family Mission and Thrift Store—Come as You Are, All Faiths Spoken Here.

"We're here, *Padre*," she announced. "We'll have you back with your people in a minute."

That didn't make sense to Carlton. If the priest was Catholic, why would he find his people at this unaffiliated mission? He was in no condition to answer questions, though.

The priest nodded silently, his eyes dull with terror. Carlton hadn't heard a coherent word out of him since the moment they'd met, and it didn't look like he would. The only thing he'd heard had been rapidly muttered prayers, not one word of which had been clear enough to make out.

Mabel got out of the van and went to the side door, then helped the priest out and guided him inside.

He was a badly shaken man. As Mabel led him across the parking lot, he didn't seem to be able to move on his own.

When Mabel let go of his hand, he just stood there, shivering like it was the middle of a Minnesota winter rather than a typical day in Miami. Mabel had to take his hand to get him to stagger to the door.

Despite her contemptuous words at the chapel, Mabel was treating the priest with a degree of sympathy. In the brief period of time during which Carlton had known her, he'd seen her display everything from cold sarcasm to ruthless brutality to empathetic kindness. She was a complicated woman.

Carlton turned to Amber. "What's the deal with Mabel?"

Amber didn't seem interested in talking, just kept her eyes glued to her phone screen as she flipped through it. Maybe she was quietly hoping for word of what had happened to Jamie.

Carlton didn't give up, though. He asked again, a little louder this time, and stared at her long enough that she had little choice but to give in.

With a huff of irritation, she replied, "I don't know much about Mabel other than that is not her real name, and she's been around for a long time. She's never aged, and she's always sent out to find new candidates to join UUE."

Carlton raised an eyebrow. "She's never aged?"

Amber shrugged. "There are a lot of theories. A few of them have been tested. A few of those testers got handed their teeth when they tried to splash Mabel with holy water or sprinkle her with garlic."

"Wait, you're telling me people suspected her of being a *vampire?*"

"Yeah, apparently. They should have kept the thought to themselves, though. You really *don't* want to see her angry."

"I'll bear that in mind," he answered. "Where's she from?"

"Are you asking if she's from Transylvania? From her accent, I'd say she's an Eastern blueblood, but who knows? Her life is defined by her mission."

"What *is* her mission?"

"Same as the rest of us. To unearth undesirable entities."

"Unearth Undesirable Entities? That's UUE. I thought UUE stood for Unexplained, Unquiet Ephemera."

She shrugged again. "SUUE stands for a lot of things. Depends on who you ask. My favorite is Sickos who Unearth Undesirable Entities."

Carlton chuckled. "What about Sad and Useless Unless Entertaining?"

"Or Sociopaths Understanding Underground Evil?" She grinned. "I'm getting ahead of myself. You're not supposed to play this game until you're one of us, and right now, it's not clear that you're going to live long enough for that to happen. Getting back to the point, Mabel's backstory is only interesting to those who've just started working for the Society. Assuming you survive long enough to put a few years behind you, you'll have seen enough weird shit to make her seem downright boring by comparison."

Carlton found that hard to imagine. Then he remembered something. The first time he'd killed a man, his cousin Jerome, who was one of the leaders in his gang, had told him it would get easier to deal with over time. Carlton had had a hard time believing it, but Jerome had been right.

The guilt had faded. The nightmares hadn't stopped, but they'd become a lot less common.

Killing *had* gotten easier. It had gotten too easy, and that was what had set him on this path. He wasn't sure he wanted to get used to all this, but his hand strayed to his wallet the way it always did, and as usual, it was enough.

It was enough to remind him of the picture he kept inside and why he had started on this path. Now that he thought about it, the wallet was the only thing he had left now that they'd abandoned the trashed safe house.

If I want to be able to protect my child, I'm going to need to be able to handle this sort of thing. Now that I know what's out there, I don't have a choice. How else am I going to learn how to do that other than by staying the course?

Mikey gave a low groan, then started seizing. His limbs flapped around like injured birds as white foam bubbled out of his mouth.

Amber spun. "Oh, shit! *Mikey!*"

She did what she could for him, but it was too late. The man was succumbing to his wounds.

"Should we call an ambulance?" Carlton asked.

Amber shook her head. "Even if we called an ambulance now, he would be dead before they got here."

Amber placed a strong and calloused hand on Mikey's face. "It's okay, Mikey. You did it. You saved Jamie from the revenants. Everything's going to be okay. You saved her, and now you can be done fighting. You did a good job."

Mikey didn't know, but his sacrifice had bought Jamie less than an hour of life. His eyes fluttered open, and he looked up into Amber's face. "Thank you...did...didn't..."

Amber nodded. "I know. You're not alone. Rest."

With that, Mikey passed. For one second, Amber's eyes teared up, and a few drops slid silently down her cheek.

She isn't as cold as she seems to be.

Carlton had seen people die before. A lot of them, and not only by his hand but in a host of different situations. For whatever reason, this death affected him more than he'd expected. He swallowed hard, finding himself caring more about this death than he had any rational explanation for.

Perhaps it was that he understood what Mikey had been feeling in those last few moments, not wanting to die alone, unnoticed and un-mourned, as though he had never existed or mattered. Amber had made sure Mikey hadn't had to face his ending alone.

Or maybe it was because Carlton understood this was his fate as well. That it was coming for him whether he'd stayed with the CIA, gone to prison, or stuck with the UUE.

Either way, like Mikey, he was going to die bloody. Watching Mikey die was like looking into his future, and if he was going to go out anyway, shouldn't he go out doing something that mattered? Something that really helped people?

If he was going to end up hemorrhaging and shuddering out his last moments in a stolen vehicle or an abandoned house, didn't he want to be doing something his kid could be proud of? He imagined his boy looking at a picture of him and feeling pride, sometime in the future when he was old enough to know about all this.

His resolve to take this job hardened despite everything he had seen. The somber moment was broken when Amber cursed and pulled out her pistol.

Carlton followed her eyes and saw that someone was walking, no, strutting, toward the van. The guy was tall and almost painfully thin, but his muscular definition could be seen since he wore no shirt under his open leather jacket.

He moved like a rockstar, and Carlton found himself

wanting to shoot the prick on general principles. The desire got stronger when he pressed his sharp-featured face to the van window. "Ah. It's you."

Carlton was ready to bring the rifle around, but Amber shook her head and moved her hand to the door. Carlton couldn't tell whether she was trying to get a clear shot or get past him.

The newcomer frowned and tsked, then put his back to the van and leaned against it.

Amber moved frighteningly quickly. Carlton had to scramble to keep up as she headed out the door. In his haste to have Amber's back, he left the rifle behind, but he had the crowbar hooked through his belt.

Amber came out of the van and came around the hood, but she seemed to hesitate to go any farther than that.

"What are you doing here, Connor?" She aimed the gun at the strange man, looking like she wanted to pull the trigger.

Old instincts died hard. His instincts told him this was a combat situation, so Carlton circled toward the back of the van, where he could be ready to act from cover. He unhooked the crowbar and kept it in hand.

Connor pulled out a blunt and lit it. The smell of potent reefer was heavy in the air as he leaned against the van. He looked for all the world like he didn't care that he had a gun pointed at him.

Connor shrugged. "I've come to meet with Mabel. Do a little information swap. I've already found out more than I expected."

Much like his swagger, every word from Connor's mouth was expressed in an arrogant, almost bored drawl.

Without looking in the back, he hooked a thumb toward Mikey's body and shook his head as he took a drag.

"Big fella's punched out, and I don't see the lovely Jamie. Given what happened at St. Ignacio's Chapel early this morning, it is not looking good. Amazing how much can change in a single night."

Amber frowned at him. "Nothing's changed."

Connor smiled ghoulishly. "Really? Caught sight of Mabel leading in a priest who looked a lot like that limp-dick fucker from St. Ignacio's. The one that made a sloppy sale of most of your hardware a few weeks ago. Do you think he would have done that if nothing had changed?"

Amber gritted her teeth. "Times get tough, and people get stupid."

Connor nodded slowly. "Unless they know they can't afford to be stupid. UUE's gone soft, and frankly, I'm disappointed. Mostly in Mabel, of course. Lady of her... austerity ought to know better."

Mabel came out of the mission in time to hear him say it.

"A gentleman of your pedigree shouldn't jump to conclusions, Connor. It could end up being a bad bet."

Connor shook his head. "You've got a compromised safe house, and that was before you kicked over an undead hornet's nest. Now two operatives are down and out, and you've got a new recruit dangling like a chunk of meat around your neck. Mabel, honey, I'm embarrassed for you."

She crossed her arms. "There's no point in denying mistakes were made. Steps were missed. We can bounce back from that. We always have."

Connor flicked the last of his blunt across the parking

lot. "'Steps were missed?' For fuck's sake, babe! I'm not sure you even understand that you're dancin'."

Mabel controlled her temper. "Well, help get me up to speed so I can stay on tempo, Connor. That's how this works, isn't it?"

Connor looked at her after a moment of consideration. "Look, there's no way I can keep my mouth shut. I'm going to have to let the word out that you're ducking out of Miami, but I'm telling you now. That means you need to pull up stakes and move north pronto. If you put enough highway between you and this shit sandwich of a city before sundown, maybe, just maybe, you've created enough of a distance to convince Ricardo his shot hasn't come yet."

Mabel's eyes flashed. "I'm not running away from that psychotic piece of shit."

Connor shrugged. It didn't matter to him. "Good luck, then. See you on the pale side because I can promise you this. Even now, some of his blood-bags are putting the pieces together. They will have something like a plan of attack before that massive leech crawls out of whatever pile of carcasses he's nesting in today. When that happens, if you are anywhere within driving distance, you are as good as dead unless you've been hiding some serious friends I haven't heard about."

Amber didn't like the sound of that. "What do you expect us to do? Just tuck tail and run?"

Connor replied in the same bored drawl. "Discretion, valor, all that shit. You figure it out."

Amber was getting agitated. "We're not bailing on Miami!"

Mabel tried to calm her. "Amber..."

Amber wheeled on Mabel. "No! Fuck him, and fuck Ricardo, too. They're right. We missed a step. We missed a step when we didn't scorched-earth every last fucking one of them."

Mabel's voice was cold and sharp. "Amber!"

As angry as she was, Amber knew enough to be quiet when she heard that tone. As for Connor, he seemed unbothered or maybe amused. The guy was insufferable.

Mabel stepped closer to Connor, almost whispering, "For all these shiny tidbits you're squawking about, what are you going to give me?"

Connor examined his fingernails. "For you? For old times' sake? I might tell everyone you were heading west instead of north. Maybe you're planning to collect yourself in New Orleans. You still have a strong hold on that city. I'll leave out that you've got fresh meat, so nobody has any reason to think you're headed to Pennsylvania."

Amber was glaring again. "Pennsylvania. Seriously? He knows too fucking much. Hell, he's probably the one who sold us out."

Mabel shook her head. "Connor's only a conduit, a channel through which things pass. If you can't keep it together, you can take a walk."

Amber was quiet again.

"Thanks, Connor." Mabel's voice wasn't friendly, but it did seem to be important to her to acknowledge what seemed like a long-standing relationship. "Be careful, and not only about Ricardo. This new necromancer is no joke. Whoever they are, they're more than just another shovel-humper. Willing to pull a full Romero within twenty-four hours of getting a grimoire and a lab torched? Somebody like that is dangerous to know."

Connor shrugged and stood up. The conversation was clearly over as far as he was concerned. "Hope to see you again, love, but not anytime soon. I'm sure that wouldn't be good for either of us."

CHAPTER EIGHT

Great, Carlton thought. *I sign up with this outfit, and they get their asses kicked and have to flee Miami!*

Mabel and Amber got back into the van, and Carlton crawled in after them. Mikey was still lying there, as dead as he'd been before.

"I assume this means we are going to be heading out of town soon?" he asked no one in particular.

Amber shook her head. Mabel looked at him in the rearview mirror. "If anything, this delays us. We would have left Miami first thing in the morning if not for the priest. Now…"

Amber finished the thought for her. "Now we have a few things we have to take care of. We'll get out of Miami after those are dealt with."

"What kinds of things?"

Amber turned to Mabel. "He asks a lot of questions, doesn't he?"

Mabel nodded. "Yes, he does. No more than most new recruits, though. Carlton, there are a few more safe houses that need to be cleaned. It's one thing if we're only leaving for a few days or if we've got people we can leave behind. It's quite another if we're leaving with no definite return date and no one watching the safe houses. In that situation, it's better to clean them out and shut them down."

Carlton remembered Mabel reaching into that shrine and smashing the clay idol. "Does it have anything to do with that little idol in the alcove?"

"That's an impressively intuitive leap," Mabel replied. "I'm not going to go into the details since that will be covered in your training, but yes. There is a…ritualistic cleansing that must be performed before we shut a safe house down. They all have an icon like the last one, and they all need to be removed in the same way to avoid…problems."

"That isn't all, though," Amber added.

Mabel glanced back into the seat at Mikey, who was staring at nothing. "No, that isn't. We don't want to be caught crossing state lines with a dead body. This is going to be a busy day. We need to get done and be well away from here before sunset."

"Like Connor told us," Amber commented bitterly.

"We're not taking orders from Connor. We're taking advice. In this case, it's solid advice. We got caught flat-footed, and we need to rebuild our strength before we'll be in a position to recapture this territory."

Amber looked away, her eyes simmering with anger.

Mabel chose not to push it. "Amber and Carlton, I'm going to task you with burying Mikey. I'll take care of the safe houses while you do that."

"Should we really be separating?" Amber asked her. "Isn't that dangerous?"

Mabel nodded. "It could be. We'll need to move quick and quiet. I want the two of you to check in with me every hour so I know you're both okay."

"What if the other safe houses are compromised?" Amber asked.

"If they are, I probably won't make it, but we can't leave them unattended."

Carlton knew then that Mabel was a commanding officer he could trust. She was willing to take the same risks she asked others to take. That was the one thing you looked for in the person who gave you orders.

Amber nodded. "Okay."

Mabel's voice was sympathetic. "Look, Amber, I know how you're feeling. We're all feeling the same way. Mikey and Jamie were our people. As soon as we get clear of this, I'll put you in charge of a new team. You'll come back to Miami with one mission: to remind every creep in this city why the UUE is not to be fucked with."

Carlton felt a chill when he heard those words. As Mabel was talking, her voice moved seamlessly from sympathetic to cold and hard. She meant what she said.

The UUE would take Miami back, and when that happened, it would be a dark day for those who had crossed the Society. And those who had stood by and let it happen.

Amber's body language changed. She sat up, revitalized and determined. "All right. Let's get rolling."

They drove a short distance before Mabel pulled over,

scanning every intersection for a sign of the enemy. When she didn't see any, she opened the van door.

"Remember. Every hour."

"You got it, Chief." Amber slid over and took the driver's seat, and Carlton moved up front to the passenger seat. Then they took off again, leaving Mabel to do what she had to do.

The promise of revenge had ignited Amber. Carlton saw that she was less down than she had been, if no less angry. Most importantly, she was moving with purpose.

Her eyes gleamed as they drove through the city, as she checked cross-streets for enemy action, as she changed gears or turned the wheel. Carlton felt energized watching her, catching her fire for vengeance.

He couldn't understand where she was going, though. Miami was on the water, so the logical thing to do was commandeer a boat, take it out into Biscayne Bay, and drop the body where no one would ever find it. Or maybe they should drive out of the city and into the Everglades, where the alligators would make short work of it.

"Hey, where are we going?" he asked. "Shouldn't we be heading for the Everglades or something?"

"You're thinking like an assassin." Her voice was hard. "Mikey was not a target. He was someone I worked with. I'm not going to dump him like a sack of garbage."

"No offense intended," he hastened to assure her.

"None taken, but I'm not looking to feed him to the gators."

"Amber, he isn't alive anymore. He doesn't care."

She glanced at Carlton. "You capable of taking orders, big guy?"

"I'm a professional if that's what you're asking."

"All right. Then why are you questioning my judgment?"

"That isn't what I'm trying to do. I just don't get it. The UUE operates in secret, right?"

"Well, yeah." She nodded. "We're a secret society. We make sure all the taxpaying citizens out there don't know anything about necromancers and revenants or any of the other things that go bump in the night."

"Right. So, if we're a secret society, don't we need to dispose of our dead comrades in a secret way? I mean, hear me out."

"Here comes the mansplaining."

He was silent, not sure how to answer that one.

"Okay, fine." She sighed. "I'll hear you out. Don't assume I'm gonna do what you want, though."

"Okay, it's like this. Mikey is gone. That isn't him in the back. It's just some meat and bones he left behind. That's all we have left. Anything he was or anything he did, if it was worth keeping, you already have it, and nothing can take it away from you. Mikey was a good guy; I can see that. And if he was, he wouldn't want you or Mabel or any of us getting busted on sentimentality."

"That's a noble sentiment." Amber didn't smile, and the words didn't sound like a compliment. "There's something you're forgetting, though."

"What's that?"

"You met your first revenant when?"

"Uh, yesterday."

"Right." She nodded. "Forty-eight hours ago, you had no

idea the dead could walk. You would have laughed if anyone told you necromancers really existed. Right?"

"That's true." He had a sinking feeling he was going to lose this argument.

"So, considering all that, how can you be so confident that all we have left here is a pile of meat and bones? I mean, you don't really know anything about it, do you?"

"Well, no. I guess not. Are you saying you…"

She shook her head. "Not gonna answer that. Let's look at one of your other points. You said Mikey was a good guy, right?"

He nodded. "Yes. I mean, he was your friend, wasn't he?"

"I never said he was my friend. I don't wanna go into details on what he was since that's complicated and irrelevant, but you can't assume that Mikey was a good guy just because he meant something to me or to anyone else."

"So, you don't think he was a good guy?"

Amber shrugged. "No one is a good guy. Revenants and necromancers? Real. Good guys? Not."

"Well, that seems…"

"I don't care what it seems like to you. Listen, there's a new ballfield being put in a few neighborhoods over. Mikey loved baseball. It's the weekend, which means the worksite will not be busy. If we could put Mikey in the foundations of one of the structures, like maybe the concessions stand, then to me, that would feel like a worthy tribute. You got me?"

He nodded. "Yeah. I got you."

Carlton hadn't changed his mind. To his operative's eye, the idea seemed dangerous and too time-intensive. When he was in the CIA, losing a guy on a mission sometimes meant leaving his body where it fell.

That might be in the desert outside a terrorist training camp. It might be deep in the jungle where no one would ever find it. It might mean dumping it in a swamp or a bay to be claimed by the water.

He was used to the idea of being left where he fell, his body treated as an inconvenience to be disposed of, but Amber was in charge and he was not.

They were not doing this for Mikey. They were doing this for Amber, so she could process the loss of her comrade and move on.

Maybe it was to process the loss of both her comrades since Jamie's body had not been recovered. This could be what Amber needed to handle it. Even if it made no sense to him to do things this way, he was one of the good guys now, and he needed to act like it.

Carlton dropped his objections, and they went to the construction site and set about putting Mikey to rest the way Amber wanted. There was nobody there, so they were able to park discreetly behind a huge pile of dirt, drop Mikey in the hole beside it, and shovel enough dirt on him so he wouldn't be spotted.

They finished by early afternoon, with Amber checking in every hour. Just before they finished, Amber's phone rang. She wiped her brow with her sleeve, then answered. "Yeah. Almost done here."

"I've done what I needed to do," Mabel replied. "Ready to meet up whenever you are."

"Okay. We'll be a little longer."

Based on what Amber said, Carlton expected them to

shovel another few feet of dirt on top of Mikey's corpse. Mikey was buried, but a body can always be a little more buried.

Instead, Amber returned the shovel they'd borrowed from the construction site. "Come on. Let's go get Mabel."

He didn't want to question her, especially after irritating her by arguing about her burial plans for Mikey. So, he didn't say anything. Instead, they got back into the car and started to drive away.

They were driving through a slightly rundown residential neighborhood, but they didn't get far before Amber pointed out the window on her left. "Did you see that?"

"No. What's up?"

She turned the van with a sudden lurch. "I just saw a little kid getting dragged into an abandoned house over there!"

"You did?"

Carlton hadn't seen that, and he didn't miss things. They were on the edge of the neighborhood, and some of the houses had scorched black walls or boarded-up windows. It bothered Carlton that he hadn't seen the kid, but he'd seen that his new coworkers were crazy strong, so maybe they were better at spotting things too.

Something felt off. It wasn't that he didn't think they should rescue a kid, but it felt like there was something he wasn't being told.

Amber screeched to a halt in front of one of the abandoned houses. If he was going to do anything about this, he needed to do it now.

"I didn't see anything, Amber. Isn't Mabel expecting us?

We don't want the necromancer to find her while we're all the way out here."

She gave him a hard look. "We aren't going to let that child be taken. Do you understand me?"

He nodded. "Yes."

"Okay, then. I'll take the upstairs. You take the downstairs."

They got out of the van and ran to the front door. Carlton tested it. "Door's locked."

"Stand aside!" she told him, and he stepped out of the way. Then she slammed her foot on the locking point and effortlessly kicked it open.

When they got through the door, Amber didn't carry out a room-clearing process like a cop or an FBI agent would. She ran up the staircase, leaving Carlton to search the downstairs by himself.

It was a nerve-wracking experience, not only because of the time crunch but also because of the memories. Moving through the empty rooms and corridors of the abandoned home was difficult, reminding him of his experiences in the basement the day before.

Every shadow seemed to loom. Every creaking board made him tense or swing around, raising his rifle. It was like being in the bathroom of that Cuban restaurant after Mabel's "test," when the waves of horror overwhelmed him.

This whole thing was weird. Amber had headed upstairs like she'd known exactly where to find what she was looking for.

That was a paranoid thought. She *had* told him she was taking the upstairs, but Carlton couldn't shake it.

There was nothing on the lower level but dust and empty rooms. The only sign he found that anyone had ever lived here was a melancholy one. On one of the doorjambs, he saw a series of red lines with children's names and different heights marked in red ink: *Elsa, Four, 40"*.

When he stopped to take a closer look, Carlton was paralyzed by a blood-curdling shriek. He didn't think it was Amber.

Whatever this was, it was not of this world. A potent spiritualist was being warned by summoned specters, and the warning was hellish.

The horrible shriek froze him in place, the first time he had ever been frozen by fear. He struggled to work up the will to rush upstairs, but a moment later, he did.

He ran to the upper level. Amber was fighting for her life, grappling a swirling mass of white clouds or flows of energy. Spirits, as far as he could tell.

"Shoot her!" yelled Amber. "Shoot the witch! It's the only way to make this stop!"

On the other side of the room, beyond the cloud of spirits, Carlton saw the witch Amber was talking about. In the grip of her power, she was terrifying, her hair flying in a ghostly wind, her skin veined with black ectoplasm, and her eyes filled with cold and spectral light.

When Carlton had seen the revenants, he'd only thought he was scared. This was much worse. The eldritch power flowing through the woman was intense and uncanny. Carlton didn't freeze this time.

When he saw that witch, his terror filled him with grim determination. This thing had to be stopped, whatever it took. He leveled his rifle, intending to shoot her in the head.

He pulled the trigger, but the cloud of spirits around Amber lashed out and bumped the rifle, throwing his aim off. The bullet tore through a wall. A moment later, the spirits slammed into the rifle again, knocking it across the room.

An ice-cold feeling went up his arm as the witch advanced, screaming in a ghostly, inhuman voice. "*GO AWAY! GO AWAY!*"

Carlton fumbled desperately for the crowbar, which was still hanging through a loop of his belt. Backing up as he reached for it, he managed to get one hand around it and pull it out as she rushed in. The weighty piece of metal hit her in the neck, snapping it.

The spirits shrieked in mourning as the witch collapsed, her body spasming as she fell. Horrified and ashamed, Carlton realized who he'd been fighting.

Not some evil creature, but a teenage girl.

Then Amber grabbed him and dragged him away. "Someone will have heard the rifle! Come on, Carlton. We need to go!"

CHAPTER NINE

They were in the van. Carlton was staring out the window, horrified. Amber was talking, but the words were just sounds to him.

"Thanks, Carlton. You saved my life in there!"

He didn't respond.

"I mean it, Carlton, you really did. But don't tell Mabel, okay? I wasn't... We weren't supposed to be there."

Carlton couldn't bring himself to talk. He couldn't make himself let go of the crowbar either. His mind was replaying a succession of gruesome images in front of his eyes. He saw himself swing that crowbar and hit a teenager in the neck, killing her instantly.

He saw himself slamming the crowbar into his own head over and over, breaking his skull like an egg. He saw his brains gush out in a wave of blood.

Come on, Carlton. Get your shit together. Yes, she was young, but you saw for yourself that she was dangerous.

He couldn't stop the images, though. They kept coming, and not all of them were about hitting himself.

Amber was still going on about the importance of keeping his mouth shut.

"I need to know you have my back on this one, Carlton. I need to know you aren't going to tell Mabel we were there."

Not only was she being pushy, but she wanted him to participate in a cover-up. He felt sick to his stomach.

He'd taken this job because he wanted to do good, but he felt like he had done something terrible. It was all Amber's fault. He'd only done what she asked him to do, and now Amber wanted him to help her sweep it under the rug.

The images of beating his head with the crowbar had morphed. He wasn't seeing himself smashing his own head now. He was seeing himself smash Amber's head.

The images were all the same. He saw her head cracking open. Saw the rush of bright red blood. He also felt a pull from the metal, a slight vibration, as if the crowbar *liked* the idea.

He wasn't going to kill anyone else, whether the crowbar wanted him to or not. He ignored her, sitting still and quiet as they drove to meet with Mabel.

When they picked Mabel up, they had to switch vehicles, which was a good thing, considering the enemy had seen them in this one.

"How'd it go?" Amber asked as if they hadn't busted into an abandoned building and killed someone.

"I did what I needed to at the safe houses," Mabel replied as they got out of the van.

She didn't look happy, and her manner seemed forced.

"What took you so long? Did you two trip over an elder horror or something?"

"You know how it goes," Amber replied evasively. "Stuff comes up."

Mabel gave Amber a long, hard look, then turned to Carlton.

"You look shellshocked, Carlton."

He didn't say anything. He hadn't said anything since they'd left the abandoned building.

Mabel eyed him. "Where's the rifle?"

The rifle was gone. It had been left behind in the abandoned building in their rush to get out before the cops showed up.

Mabel turned to Amber with a clenched jaw. When she spoke, her voice was cold and hard, a study in controlled fury. "Are you kidding me?"

Amber fumbled for an explanation. "Come on, Mabel. It was nothing. Just a little side job. Nothing relevant to what's going on right now. See, we were going by that neighborhood where..."

"Just be silent. I'll deal with you later, but I need you both in the vehicle *right now*."

Regular Mabel was frightening, but pissed-off Mabel was traumatizing. Amber scurried into the vehicle, and Carlton climbed into the back and leaned his head against the window.

He was going to get over this. He knew he would. It was like Jerome had told him. Over time, you could get used to anything. He only had to get that image of the girl's neck snapping out of his mind.

As they tore away and headed north, the atmosphere in the vehicle was tense and heavy. Carlton got the feeling that the recent disaster had been a long time coming. That something had been causing increased tension in the Miami branch for a while. Now the branch had been all but wiped out, and everyone was looking for someone to blame.

They were on Interstate 95, so Carlton figured they were heading for Pennsylvania. It was getting dark, and headlights were coming on around them. Mabel remained coldly silent for a while, but it didn't take long for the argument to start.

"Do you understand what you did?" she asked.

"That's a little melodramatic, don't you think? Hunting creeps is what I do. The way I figure it, I did my job."

Mabel shook her head. "Your job is not just hunting creeps. Your job is to hunt them in a particular way, according to the protocols of the Society. According to the chain of command."

"What's the big deal, Mabel? We didn't lose anyone. The op was a success."

"The op was *unsanctioned.* That's the only thing that matters. You aren't an agent. You're only an operative. You *do not* have the authority to sanction ops. I need you to tell me exactly what happened."

"Okay, okay." Amber threw her hands up. "I can tell you that. You know that girl we were watching? The spiritualist?"

Mabel nodded. "Yes. Not a serious threat to anyone, just a teenage girl dabbling in spirit control. An unpopular, not conventionally attractive young woman. What about her?"

Mabel was emphasizing that the girl was not a real

threat and they shouldn't have gone after her. Carlton sank down into the back seat.

"Come on, Mabel," Amber responded. "It isn't like that. That girl was using wayward specters and spirits to get petty revenge on her classmates. That's why you assigned us to watch her, that and because she had a lot of power potential. She was leveling up, and you know she was. She'd been indulging in more dangerous stuff."

"I note you're talking about her in the past tense. That tells me your error is worse than I thought. You didn't only take Carlton into a situation he wasn't prepared for. You also determined you were going to kill a target without going through the SOS protocol mandated by the Society."

Carlton perked up when he heard that, but he didn't say anything. He was not ready to speak. Mabel noticed, though, and gave him an explanation.

"The UUE doesn't just give us a license to kill," she told him. "Killing has to be in self-defense, or it has to follow the SOS protocol. That's a three-stage process—Self, Others, and Society. Self. Are they a danger to themselves? If that's all it is, we aren't going to kill them. We'll watch them and try to determine whether we need to intervene. Others. Are they a danger to others? If they are, we might need to kill to prevent greater harm. Society. Do they threaten to reveal the truth about the supernatural to society at large? That's the case in which we're most likely to eliminate a target. We don't want anyone pulling away the veil."

"There you have it," Amber told her. "This killing was in self-defense, a straightforward case."

"Except that you broke into the target's dwelling. How

is that self-defense? In any case, you aren't authorized to run an SOS protocol. That requires at least two initiates ranked as agent or higher unless there is a direct and obvious threat."

Carlton didn't want what they'd done to be totally unauthorized. That made it worse. He finally found his voice. "Amber…Amber saw someone dragging a kid into that abandoned building."

When he heard the words, they didn't sound believable even to him. He hadn't seen a kid, and they hadn't found any kids when they went inside. Amber squirmed uncomfortably, and Carlton realized she'd made the whole thing up.

This was a target she had wanted to move on, and she'd lied to him to get him to help. She was only supposed to be surveilling the girl.

Amber wasn't ready to admit she'd done anything wrong.

"Look," she countered, "maybe I saw something that wasn't there. We've been under a lot of stress, but that girl went up there like she's been doing weekend after weekend because she wanted to indulge in petty revenge magic against rivals at school and in her neighborhood. It was only a matter of time before she killed someone. By putting a stop to it, who knows how many lives we saved?"

"That's a bullshit argument," Mabel snapped. "You can't go preemptively killing spiritualists on the theory that they *might* end up hurting someone. That's a witch hunt!"

Amber *had* described the girl as a witch. Carlton got angrier.

"Was I a little quick on the trigger? I guess I was."

Amber shrugged. "You know what, though? I think that's okay. I think if we'd been quicker on the trigger a little more often, we wouldn't always be chasing our tails. If we met any hint of trouble with a fucking firestorm, maybe the creeps of this city would be *scared* of the UUE. You know, the way they *used* to be?"

Mabel answered like she thought Amber was talking nonsense. "So, if we ruled by fear and instituted a reign of terror on the streets of Miami, you believe we'd have better control of the city?"

"Yeah, I do. You know what? I really do. If we had them running scared, the situation we're in right now would not have happened. Jamie and Mikey would not be dead."

She started shaking, and a tear rolled down her cheek. Carlton didn't know what to think. Amber was out of control, and she'd manipulated him into doing something he would regret for the rest of his life. She was also clearly traumatized and making bad decisions as a result.

The two of them were so caught up in their argument they didn't notice the headlights behind them. As the accusations and counterarguments went back and forth, the vehicle following them steadily advanced. It would catch up with them, then fall back, catch up and fall back.

Anyone watching it would have said it was keeping tabs on them. For an experienced operator like Carlton, it should have been obvious. Unfortunately for all of them, he was distracted.

His new boss's anger was both seething and cold. His coworker had lied and manipulated him. He'd *killed* someone and didn't feel good about it.

He was far too experienced to be distracted for long,

though. As they came by an on-ramp, another vehicle joined the first, then a third vehicle joined the other two. Carlton picked up that they were being tailed.

They were driving on a lonely stretch of highway, and every vehicle around them had joined their pursuit.

"Hey, uh, Mabel?" he began. "Do you see all the vehicles around us? I don't mean to interrupt, but it looks to me like we're being followed. That's what my instincts tell me, anyway."

Mabel looked in the rearview mirror, where the headlights were clearly driving in loose formation. It looked like a post-apocalyptic raiding party.

One car sped up and roared close to them, pulling even with their left rear bumper. Another did the same to their rear bumper on the right.

As for the car directly behind them, it revved its engine and came in until it was inches away and still speeding up. There was no longer any doubt. They *were* being pursued.

Somebody was not content to let the UUE retreat from Miami. Whoever they were, they wanted to wipe the Miami branch of the Society off the face of the Earth.

"Goddammit!" Mabel exclaimed. "They're on us like a revenant on a chunk of fresh meat. Brace yourselves. I'm going to hammer it!"

Carlton braced as Mabel suggested, and she floored it. Their vehicle leaped ahead and roared down the highway ahead of their pursuers.

The highway was straight, with no sudden turns. That meant the outcome of the chase would be determined by the other vehicles and their drivers' willingness to drive fast.

Mabel had no qualms when it came to speed. She white-knuckled it down the highway with the convoy of pursuers behind her, and she never seemed to think about slowing down.

Unfortunately, the pursuit cars had more powerful motors. They fell behind when Mabel sped up, but then they were on her bumper again, almost boxing her in.

The roar of their powerful engines sounded like a pride of angry lions, and it looked to Carlton like they weren't going to make it. Mabel didn't let up on the gas pedal. The pursuers not only kept pace, but they also started to gain.

Since they were on Mabel's rear bumper, that was bad. The vehicle on the left pulled alongside them, and the vehicle on the right crowded them from that side.

The car behind them tapped their bumper, causing Mabel to swerve and almost lose control. The only thing keeping her from going off the highway at speed was that she was hemmed in on either side.

Glancing at the front seat, Carlton saw Mabel was in control of herself, even if she was barely in control of her vehicle. Amber, as hard as she acted, was terrified, and Carlton could hardly blame her. They were going so fast that any mistake would be fatal.

When the vehicle on their left crept up beside them, Carlton could see into it. His jaw dropped at the crazy sight that met his eyes.

The driver of the slick and expensive sports car looked like an extra in a death metal video. He was wearing a leather jacket and racing down the highway like he didn't care if he lived or died, and that was only the tip of the iceberg.

On the front of the car, a person had been spread-eagled as if they were being crucified St. Andrews style. Naked to the whipping wind, they looked like a human sacrifice.

Crouching on top of the vehicle was a heavily muscled man with long dark hair streaming behind him. Carlton couldn't begin to understand how he stayed up there effortlessly rather than being thrown to his death.

As Carlton stared, mouth hanging open, the man laughed like this scene was the best joke he had ever told.

That guy is insane. He's crazy.

"I gotta give him this," Amber commented. "He knows how to make an impression."

Mabel turned for a quick look, and her face went pale.

"Fuck, no. That's Ricardo!" Then she saw the man sprawled on the hood and cursed even louder. "*GODDAMN THEM ALL!* He's crucified Connor!"

Carlton looked closer. She was right. The person strapped to the hood of the car *was* Connor.

He wasn't doing so well. He looked like he'd been badly beaten since his narrow chest was covered in welts. From the look of the welts, he'd been beaten with a whip or a braided wire. They'd covered his whole body with ugly red marks.

He hung on the hood of the car, eyes half-open, his chest rising and falling raggedly. The man was half-alive, and the remaining time he had was filled with terrible suffering.

Carlton hadn't liked him and had wanted to give him a solid smack. He hadn't wanted this, though. He wouldn't wish a fate like this on anybody.

Their car was still rocketing down the highway, and the cars chasing them were keeping up. Mabel let go of the steering wheel with one hand and fished out her handgun.

"Shoot the bastards!"

"You don't have to tell me twice," Amber replied. She rolled down her window, then wiggled half out of it until she was sitting up, facing Ricardo's car. Carlton rolled his window down as well, and they both started shooting.

It might have made sense to shoot the driver, but Carlton felt like he should target Ricardo. It wasn't easy to hit a moving target from inside a vehicle, but Carlton was sure his shots were landing.

Amber was leaning out as far as she dared, trying to get her weapon lined up. Her shots were landing as well. Carlton could see the impacts on Ricardo's body when they hit.

The only problem was that Ricardo didn't seem to care. He crouched on top of the car like getting shot wasn't an inconvenience.

From Ricardo's reaction, he took being shot multiple times as a personal challenge. He laughed wildly as the bullets slammed into him, then slapped his hand on the roof hard. The sports car veered sharply and crashed into their car.

Carlton was later amazed that he could still remember any of it. As it was, he remembered only a series of terrifying snapshots, each one vague and unreal.

The impact of Ricardo's car as it smashed into their car from the side.

A flash of light, bright and disorienting.

Sparks.

The feeling of veering out of control and shooting off the highway at high speed.

Losing contact with the earth and soaring through the air like a bird.

The moment before they hit the ground when the car arced down again, it became obvious that they were going to land nose-first. Carlton was able to remember anticipating the impact but not the impact itself.

He breathed in sharply, a panic reaction, and the car dove at the ground like a swimmer jumping headfirst into a pool. Then there was nothing but a void, his memories erased as if he had disappeared off the face of the planet.

CHAPTER TEN

Carlton came to, not knowing where he was or what he was doing there. He didn't know how long he'd been out, and it took a few minutes before his brain was able to access the disconnected images from before the crash.

All he knew was that he was in a car and that the car appeared to have suffered a lot of damage. He couldn't understand how he was alive.

What had he been doing in a car? He had the vague sense that he'd been driving to Pennsylvania, although he couldn't remember why. Was that where he was?

No. The night air didn't feel anything like Pennsylvania. It felt warm and humid. It felt like Florida, the place he'd been living while he applied for the FBI as part of his plan to impress Marly.

Except that he hadn't been hired by the FBI. He'd been hired by a woman named Mabel who had locked him in a basement with way too many angry dead people.

It all came back to him, including flashes from before the crash. Carlton knew where he was, and he knew he needed to drag himself out of the wreckage before it caught fire and burned him alive.

He reached out blindly and was surprised to feel his hand close around the crowbar. That thing wasn't easy to get rid of. Having said that, it would be helpful.

Once he had it in his hand, he battered away the jagged debris in front of him. When he found it hard to move, he used the crowbar like a cane, bracing himself to push his body upward. With its help, he was able to crawl out the shattered window on the passenger side and drop onto the grass.

He looked at the highway and saw a mangled guard rail. They must have come through it, although he couldn't remember that happening. He had a mental image of Amber hanging out of the window, then being thrown clear the way a child would toss a ragdoll.

Carlton wasn't sure where that memory fit with the others. He had no idea what had happened to Mabel and couldn't see her as he struggled clear of the wreck.

He emerged below the glare of headlights and caught a glimpse of figures standing along the twisted guardrail at the edge of the highway. They were looking toward the wreck.

From nearby, he heard a groan and turned to see that Connor was still alive, as impossible as that seemed. The man was still strapped to the hood of the sportscar, which had half its hood (and thus half of Connor) wedged into the side of Carlton's vehicle.

Mabel was next to him, talking softly, though Carlton wasn't sure whether she was comforting or asking questions.

Connor was whispering back. How the hell were both of them still alive? The car must have been going a hundred miles an hour when it hit.

Carlton's attention was drawn back to the edge of the road. Ricardo had dragged a squirming and kicking form forward and pitched it down the slope like it was a sack of trash. The figure bounced and rolled down the slope and came to rest near Carlton with a faint moan.

It turned out to be Amber, the most impossible survivor of all. Despite being thrown from a moving vehicle at high speed, then dropped off a hill, she seemed intact, though she was in quite a bit of pain. Carlton imagined she had sprained joints and broken bones, but she was clearly alive.

Not a single person in their vehicle had been killed in the catastrophic crash. Based on the figures on the road, no one in the sports car had been killed either.

Everyone was fine, although that couldn't last much longer. Their pursuers had not come here to let them walk away alive.

Slowly but confidently, Ricardo walked down the slope, followed by his entourage. A light still shone crookedly from one of the totaled vehicles, and it fell on Ricardo's face as he advanced.

Carlton didn't have to ask what Ricardo was. He'd had hints, but when he got a look at the man's face, it was obvious.

Ricardo's eyes reminded Carlton of a feral dog that had lived in his neighborhood when he was a child. The dog had kept to the shadows and eaten scraps. If you got near it, it would bark like it wanted to eat your face off, its eyes demented and hungry. Ricardo's features looked cruel and inhuman, although it wasn't easy to say why.

The giveaway came when Ricardo opened his mouth. His canine teeth were unnaturally long and tapered to sharp points.

Ricardo was a vampire.

"So, Mabel," Ricardo taunted. "You sent your little magpie out to tell everyone lies. Unfortunately for you, I can spot a lie from a thousand miles away. You cannot fool me! When your magpie chirped, I knew what you were up to. Poor Connor had to tell the truth, even if he tried to avoid it. As you can see, there are consequences for lying to me!"

"Stop playing games, Ricardo," Mabel countered. "You're a liar too. The biggest liar of all."

"Did you think I was making a moral argument?" Ricardo smiled in amusement, revealing his long, cruel fangs. "Don't be ridiculous! I'm not saying I never lie. I'm saying there are consequences when others lie to *me*, as Connor found out. He was eager to tell the truth in the end, and now I can make you pay for what you did."

"All right. You're not a hypocrite, just a predator." Mabel rose from Connor's side and approached, stopping when she reached Carlton.

Unafraid, she looked Ricardo in the eyes. "Yes, I killed Lucien."

His eyes blazed as he bared his fangs, but he didn't seem to dare get too close.

"I know he was your lover," Mabel continued, "But he was out of control. Even the other vampires knew it. That was why they made it easy for me to take him down."

"That is a filthy lie! His own kind would not have turned on him."

"Oh, but they did, Ricardo. It's hardly the first time your people have given up one of their own to the UUE. You vampires love to speak poetically about your loyalty to your own, but the reality is you are self-serving monsters. You can't expect much from a monster, as Lucien discovered. When he went too far and endangered his people, they were all ready to turn their backs on him."

Ricardo didn't say anything, but his eyes filled with hatred. He seemed to be struggling to decide whether to attack.

Mabel pressed her advantage. "If you can make your peace with that, maybe you'll live a little longer. If you cannot, you're going to end up like Lucien. It's your decision, Ricardo. No one can make it for you."

"My decision?" he spat. "My decision was made when you killed my Lucien!"

He took a step in her direction, but Amber fired into him point-blank. She pulled the trigger again and again, the muzzle flashes looking like bursts of lightning.

She aimed for Ricardo's heart at first, but the vampire twisted his upper body with inhuman speed to make sure none of her shots hit the target. The bullets blasted holes in his flesh, but his unnatural healing powers closed the holes as quickly as they formed.

Carlton gaped as he saw the holes appear and disappear in Ricardo's torso. Now he understood the meaning of the word "undead." Ricardo wasn't alive, so being shot meant little to him. Unless Amber managed to hit him in a vulnerable spot, it was like shooting a slab of meat at the butcher's. Worse than that, he could heal his body almost instantly.

Amber tried to aim at his head, but he dodged every one of these shots as well, his face blurring as he twisted back and forth, back arching as he leaned away.

A few seconds later, Amber emptied her magazine without landing a single shot that counted. Ricardo was unharmed, but the attempt to kill him had made him even angrier.

As Amber reached for another magazine, Ricardo grabbed her by the throat. He lifted her off her feet one-handed and dangled her in front of him.

"Stupid child!" he spat. "Do you think I am like a fledgling, to be killed so easily?"

Carlton thought he would drink her blood and started forward to do something about it. He might not be able to fight a vampire who could easily dodge bullets, but he couldn't let a comrade in arms die without trying to help.

Not even one who had lied to him and manipulated him. Mabel stopped him, urgently shaking her head. Carlton stopped, expecting Ricardo to sink his teeth into Amber.

Ricardo didn't try to drink from her. Instead, he hurled her away from him like he was repulsed by the thought of her. She flew, pinwheeling in panic, then slammed into the ground. There she remained, unconscious or dead.

Ricardo was stronger than his muscular body suggested.

"I promise you this, Mabel," he announced. "You are all going to die slowly. No simple bloodletting but a feast of pain. You say I am nothing but a predator, but you have no concept of the pain I have experienced since Lucien was killed. Even though I intend to kill you slower than I have killed any other human being, you will experience only a fraction of the suffering I have experienced."

Carlton laughed out loud, and the vampire's head swiveled in his direction.

"You are not wise to make me notice you, novice," Ricardo told him.

"I'm sorry, buddy," Carlton replied. "It's just that I'd never have guessed a real vampire would be as emo as the ones in the movies. But hey, you do you. Layer on the melodrama. Go right ahead."

Ricardo growled like an angry beast, again reminding Carlton of that feral dog from his childhood. The vampire's eyes filled with wild rage, but he did not step forward. Carlton couldn't help but think Ricardo was scared of them or what they were capable of.

"Oh, quit it, Ricardo," Mabel told him. "Carlton's right. Vampires are the biggest crybabies in the supernatural world."

She produced a syringe filled with bronze liquid. Ricardo's eyes were drawn to it like he knew he should be afraid of it. Nevertheless, he mocked her.

"One of your potions? You're delusional, Mabel. You just saw me dodging bullets at point-blank range. What makes you think you'll get a chance to put one of your concoctions in me before I rip your arms off your body?"

"You're probably right, Ricardo. But this concoction isn't for you."

A moment later, Carlton found out why she hadn't

wanted him to move on Ricardo. She lunged sideways, grabbed his arm, and jabbed the syringe into him.

He was so surprised that he didn't move, and the needle went into him so smoothly that he hardly felt it. Mabel depressed the plunger, and Carlton's body burned as if he were filled with acid.

Ricardo screamed in unholy rage and lunged after Mabel, shrieking to his followers. "Kill them! Kill them all! Kill the filthy animals!"

Carlton barely heard him, and a dissociative part of his mind that wasn't shrieking in agony took a moment to note he probably wouldn't have to worry about being killed by vampire minions. He had never been in this much pain in his life, and it was going to kill him horribly before the minions got a chance to.

It felt like he was being burned at the stake if you had first been bathed in acid. It felt like his skin ought to be melting off, but he didn't see anything wrong with it. If he was really being burned alive, it should have stopped hurting when his nerve endings burned away, which should have happened by now.

The burning continued.

These thoughts felt like they took an eternity because of the intense pain. In reality, they took only a moment—the time needed for Ricardo to rush past Carlton to get to Mabel, who was retreating.

As Ricardo ran by, he knocked Carlton over with a shoulder bump. The impact was like getting clipped by a car while stepping off the curb, except Carlton could hardly feel it.

He spun and hit the ground like a dropped piano. The

sensation of slamming into the earth made Carlton understand something he hadn't been able to before.

The reason his skin wasn't melting was that he *wasn't* burning. The sensation was neither acid nor fire but rage. Pure, undiluted *fury*.

He'd been angry before, angry enough to kill, although killing for him was generally more a matter of professional duty than anger. No rage he had ever experienced could compare to this, and that was why it felt like a raging fire consuming his body. If he used that anger, tapped into it and let it flow through him freely, there wouldn't be a creature on Earth capable of stopping him.

Not even a vampire.

With the rage coursing through him, that shove from Ricardo was like setting off a bomb. He had dropped the crowbar when he fell, but he reached down and snatched it up again.

With the crowbar in his hand, he could feel its hunger. He could feel its need to pummel flesh and snap bones. To turn a human body into a dripping liquid mess.

Screaming like a feral animal, Carlton charged Ricardo, whose back was turned as he attacked Mabel. He slammed the crowbar into Ricardo's exposed back, then looped around and slammed it again. Ricardo didn't react, though the impact of the crowbar staggered him. He was too focused on trying to kill Mabel.

Carlton just kept hammering away. He didn't know how many times he hit Ricardo, but the vampire eventually dropped flat beneath the impact. Even a body as dead and insensitive as Ricardo's could be physically beaten to the ground, and that was what Carlton was doing.

As Ricardo fell, he twisted like a worm on a hook. Target blindness had left the vampire vulnerable, but he kept some of his supernatural agility despite having taken a dozen heavy hits.

He tried to turn, but the crowbar hit him in the jaw. Ricardo fell again, driven to the ground by repeated impacts. Carlton kept hitting him, the rage burning inside him turning everything to red and mottled black.

Though Ricardo was no longer moving, Carlton raised the crowbar and brought it down, raised it again and brought it down. He was dimly aware that the vampire's wounds were healing rapidly, but he hit the thing so many times that new wounds appeared before the old wounds could heal.

His urge to kill was uncontrollable.

Ricardo was out of the fight, but his minions were not. Carlton no longer cared about the minions, however. He was no longer thinking about vampires. He only wanted to kill, and it no longer mattered who or why.

Their mere presence was enough. When a figure loomed up in his field of vision, he battered it with the crowbar until the figure stopped moving or until something else appeared and distracted him.

Every fiber of his being, physical, mental, and emotional, was bent on one thing—swinging the bludgeon over and over as hard as he could.

A vampire jumped at him, and he hit it so hard that he cracked the thing's skull. It staggered and fell sideways, blood oozing from a gaping head wound.

Another vampire tried to tackle him, and he slammed

the bottom of the crowbar through the top of the monster's head, causing it to collapse to its knees.

A pair of vampires tried to grab him, and he took them both out in an X-shaped strike pattern, the one on the right followed immediately by the one on the left. They both staggered and fell, and he kept hitting them until there was nothing left of their skulls.

At some point, he realized there was nothing else to hit. Nothing else to vent his fury on. He stopped and looked down at the crowbar, intending to go on killing as soon as he caught his breath.

When he glanced at the hunk of metal, he saw a cold and spectral light beneath the slick layer of blood, hair, skin, and fragments of torn clothing that covered it.

He watched it, mesmerized. It was beautiful, like a distant voice singing on a lonely moor. Carlton couldn't understand why his crowbar was glowing, but he didn't need to. He'd seen so many unheard-of things in the past day that a crowbar glowing with an eldritch beauty didn't stand out from the crowd.

As he stared at the light, Carlton's rage faded. A moment ago, he'd been killing without caring who or what he killed. If Mabel or Amber had been in front of him, he'd have beaten them to a blood-soaked pulp as happily as he'd beaten the vampires.

Now the deranged fury was draining out of him since the only thing he could focus on was the cold light.

I've seen that light before.

He'd seen it in the abandoned building when he'd faced off with the young woman in the grip of the spirits. The light reminded him of her unnatural gaze as the spirits swarmed over Amber and the girl advanced on him, moaning like a ghost for him to go away.

Her glowing eyes seemed to be trapped in the depths of the crowbar's iron.

The light rushed forward and slammed against the interior of the iron like a prisoner throwing their body weight against the bars of their prison. The crowbar jumped in his hands and Carlton dropped it. It clattered when it hit a rock on the ground.

For a long moment, all Carlton could do was stand and listen to the echo of the dropped crowbar hitting the rock. It sounded like a blacksmith striking his anvil, leaving a lingering echo.

With the crowbar no longer in his hand, Carlton looked around. He felt he could not have done so a moment earlier.

He blinked several times, then closed his eyes, trying to get his mind around what had happened. Had he killed several vampires as they rushed to attack him, or had he killed innocent people because he'd gone mad with a crowbar?

He opened his eyes and looked around, hoping to answer this question.

There were several dead bodies on the ground. Some were so badly pulverized that it was hard to say they were human. As he'd imagined while he was swinging the crowbar, he'd reduced these bodies to a condition closer to liquid than solid.

He didn't see remains that looked like they belonged to Ricardo. Despite his efforts to beat the vampire into a sloppy mess, Ricardo had managed to slip away.

His followers hadn't managed. They'd been beaten so badly that there was not much left of them, just little bits sticking up out of the gore. Carlton recognized a shard of rib, something that might have been a skull, and...

He couldn't identify whether the dead had been humans or vampires. There wasn't enough left of them.

The whole scene was beyond horrific, but Carlton couldn't bring himself to react. He stared at the bodies with distant, neutral eyes.

I ought to be puking my guts out. I ought to feel bad about this, but I can't feel a thing. Maybe I'm too tired.

He turned his head, scanning the environment for any change. He saw that Connor was gone, with no sign that he had been there except a streak of blood on the hood of the car.

Mabel approached him cautiously like he was a wounded animal. Part of him understood why she might not want to get too close. If she had survived that berserk rampage, she must have seen the whole thing, meaning she might think of him as a monster worse than the vampires he had destroyed.

Carlton looked down at his hands, not surprised to see that they were raw and trembling.

What happened to me? What did I become?

"It's okay, Carlton," Mabel called. "These are all expected side effects. Whatever you're thinking right now, whatever you're feeling, I want you to know others have felt the same things."

"I-I don't know what happened..."

"I *do* know what happened, and I assure you there is nothing wrong with you. I'll explain it later, but you can take my word for it. You haven't become a monster or anything like that. In an important sense, you could say you just experienced what it was like to be completely human. Human in a way your ancestors once were and have not been for many thousands of years."

Carlton blinked at her. "What?"

"I'll explain later. For now, you should probably sit down."

He blinked at her again. "What?"

"Sit down, Carlton!"

He looked at the crazy scene. Two wrecked cars were more or less fused together. Multiple dead bodies were scattered among the wreckage. Tongues of bright orange flame flickered among shards of twisted metal and piles of broken glass.

What did it matter whether he was sitting or standing? This was the apocalypse, wasn't it?

He turned toward Mabel, still confused. "Why?"

Before Mabel could answer, he fell, the ground rushing up at him with disconcerting speed. When he hit the ground, Carlton's world went black.

Mabel stood above him, shaking her head. "Goddammit! Why don't these guys *ever* listen?"

From the wreckage, Amber stood and made her way over. She was unsteady on her feet but nowhere near as badly injured as she should have been. Amber had taken being thrown from a car, pushed down a steep slope, and tossed through the air by a heavily muscled vampire in her stride.

"He didn't listen 'cause he's a dummy. Good thing you

got that concoction into him. That one was a little closer than I'd have liked."

Mabel nodded. "I'm afraid it was. Help me get him into one of the cars up there. We have a lot of miles to cover by dawn."

CHAPTER ELEVEN

When Carlton woke up, he was in the back of an unfamiliar car. He blinked his eyes open and saw daylight, then quickly closed them. It was too soon. He wasn't ready to look at the world.

That wasn't all. Where was he? When he'd opened his eyes, he'd seen he was in a car, but the car they'd been driving had been totaled when Ricardo's vehicle rammed it. Where had they gotten this vehicle?

The car smelled like cologne. English Leather, maybe? No, that was a mental association. He was smelling cheap cologne combined with too much leather cleaner.

As far as Carlton could tell without opening his eyes, he was in the car of a man who spent a lot of time at a casino. Not a high-class establishment, either. Someplace tacky.

Where would Mabel have found another car? He didn't think she would have carjacked a passing motorist, although he couldn't be sure. Mabel was not a benevolent person.

It didn't seem the most likely explanation, though.

No, she must have taken one of the vampires' surviving vehicles. He was sprawled in the back of a vampire car, feeling like he had one hell of a hangover.

At least he'd slept, for what that was worth. Considering the pain behind his eyes and the thick, dry feeling in his throat, he would be at death's door if he hadn't slept.

Carlton slowly opened his eyes again, confirming that Mabel was driving the car and Amber was sitting in the passenger seat next to her.

What the hell was Amber doing there? The woman wouldn't die. He should have known better than to assume otherwise, considering how much he'd seen her survive the night before.

She was on the passenger side of the car, shifting uncomfortably but looking fine. With all the abuse she'd suffered, she should be dead or crippled for life. Carlton didn't understand why she wasn't, but it didn't seem like the time to ask.

"Shouldn't you be dead?" was not a great conversation starter.

Thinking about the abuse he'd seen her suffer, Carlton remembered his hands. He held them up for inspection and saw that while they were still raw from the workout he'd put them through, they were much closer to being healed than he'd expected.

One mystery after another, but one thing was clear. They'd survived the attack on the highway and were still on the road to Pennsylvania.

He closed his eyes again, thinking he'd doze for another minute, then wake up for real and find out what was going on. It didn't work out that way. When he closed his eyes, he drifted back into a deep sleep.

This time he had a whimsical dream in which he was beating vampires with a gigantic crowbar. Every time he hit one of them on the head, a chime sounded, and an ice cream cone popped out of its mouth.

Coming out of that dream into reality was disconcerting, especially when he remembered that he really had hit vampires with a crowbar. He caught sight of the crowbar. Someone had grabbed it before bundling him into the car, and it was sitting on the floor, waiting for future use.

"How long have I been out?" he asked hoarsely.

"The better part of eight hours," Mabel replied.

"That doesn't make sense. My hands haven't had time to heal this much." He held them up for a closer look, marveling at how rapidly the damage was fading.

Mabel explained, "We're still heading north to Pennsylvania. Susquehannock State Forest. The Society's headquarters is there. What should have happened was that we went there, you were sedated properly, and the infusion I gave you earlier would have been administered. It wasn't supposed to happen the way it did, but Ricardo forced my hand."

"That's oddly reassuring."

Amber turned to look at him. "Why in the world is that reassuring?"

"Because it means she isn't planning to stick me with a needle and pump me full of an incredibly painful murder drug every time we get attacked by vampires. There's a sentence that has probably never been said in human history."

"I wouldn't be so sure," replied Amber.

Mabel continued. "If you'd received the infusion at the proper time, your body would have had a chance to come to grips with the changes it produces. The infusion is formulated to awaken the primal vitality, strength, and speed that humans once had to help them survive in a world full of creatures that go bump in the night. This was before civilizations and the veil of secrecy about supernatural matters made such things not only unnecessary but counterproductive for human survival."

"So, that was basically a caveman infusion?"

"You could call it that, yes. In any case, the infusion is known to cause extreme side effects. We refer to these as primal shock. The severity of one's primal shock is dependent on a number of factors, but it is good that you are so fit since I was fairly confident your body could handle the strain."

"Fairly confident, huh? That's reassuring. What would have happened if I hadn't handled the strain?"

"We wouldn't have needed to go to Pennsylvania."

From the flatness of her tone, he understood how it was. If he hadn't been able to handle the strain, the infusion would have killed him. It was nice to know some things about his chosen career remained the same. He might be battling hungry revenants and beating angry vampires with a crowbar, but his employer still considered him expendable.

"Okay. I survived the primal shock, and I've been infused with essence of caveman. Now what?"

Amber chuckled. "Come on, Carlton. You weren't that far from being a caveman before we met you."

"Fair enough."

Mabel went on. "There are still issues that will need to be worked out with the infusion. Like, tailoring the chemical reactions to your body's needs, and that sort of thing. In the meantime, you should expect it to feel like you're going through puberty again. Raging hormones and all that. It might not be comfortable, but I promise we will get that all ironed out when we get to headquarters."

Raging hormones? Great. And here I am, traveling with two women.

"Okay. What about after, when the transition is over? What will my new normal look like?"

Amber gave a self-satisfied smirk. "Me."

Carlton gave her a flat look. "I'm going to look like you?"

"Hey, don't knock it. Like it or not, this is what peak performance looks like."

"You won't look like Amber," Mabel hastened to reassure him. "You'll probably look mostly the same as you do now. Some things won't change, of course, but some things will. You'll have an increased appetite. You might bulk up with muscle or slim down a little. It's all about finding a new equilibrium, and that's different for everyone since everyone has a different body. It might not turn out to be all that extreme."

"I'm noticing a lot of uncertain statements."

"What do you mean?" she asked.

"You say that it may not turn out to be too extreme, but that means that it *might*. What would it look like if it turns out extreme?"

She shrugged. "Who knows? You might become incredibly muscular. I've seen that happen. Your metabolism might go haywire, forcing you to consume huge amounts of calories without letting you gain weight. You might become promiscuous."

He raised his eyebrows. "Promiscuous? Why would the caveman infusion make me promiscuous?"

"It's a matter of hormones. Even without an extreme reaction, most members have elevated hormone levels for some time after receiving the infusion, especially testosterone. That's all well and good for you. Most guys are happy to have an extra shot of the man juice. On the other hand, it's a proper pain in the ass for a gal wanting to wear a cute pencil skirt and killer heels. I used to go through razors like chewing gum."

"'Man juice?'" asked Amber. "Really?"

Carlton agreed. "That is a terrible thing to call it."

"She's only teasing," Amber told him. "Mabel *does* have a sense of humor, but unfortunately, it's a *bad* sense of humor. Kind of like someone who tells dad jokes all the time with a deadpan expression, except none of the jokes are funny."

"Ouch," Mabel replied, "and no. I don't have a sense of humor of any kind." She paused for a long moment before continuing in a quieter voice. "Not even chuckle-funny?"

Amber shook her head. "Not even awkward smile-funny. Not even awkward smile with desperate urge to escape-funny."

"Well."

"No offense," Amber added.

"None taken."

The exchange made everything awkward, so Carlton

wasn't eager to resume the conversation. He sat in the back seat as the miles rolled by, watching the cars filled with commuters or vacationing families, the tractor-trailers, and the occasional turkey vulture.

He was still curious about the caveman infusion, though. They had given him a drug that made him the physical equal of several vampires. No, scratch that. Their physical *superior*.

Maybe it wouldn't be as dramatic as time went by. Maybe it would be an advantage when he got in a fight or had to move a big pile of heavy boxes or something. Or maybe it would always make him a Stone Age superman. He didn't know.

He *was* curious, and he wasn't willing to let it drop.

"How do they make the infusion?" Carlton asked.

Mabel gave him a wink in the rearview mirror. "That's a trade secret. You might get to learn more about it in time, but for now, that's not information you can have access to."

Another reassuring continuity from his former life. "The CIA was always keeping secrets from me too. The more things change..."

"Well, there *is* a reason we picked you," Mabel told him. "We like to work with former Special Forces operators, intelligence agents, and so on. They are good at keeping secrets, taking orders without understanding them, and that sort of thing."

"Understood. Is there *anything* you can tell me about it?"

"I can tell you the history. It was discovered shortly after WWII by research-oriented members of the UUE. While conducting research on a remote ring of Pacific islands, they discovered a substance with remarkable properties."

"Crazy stuff," Amber qualified.

"Yes. Crazy stuff. That was the origin of the primal infusion."

"I see. Well, based on my experience, the stuff needs to be refined. I've never felt anything like that in my life."

Amber nodded sympathetically. "Burns like hell, doesn't it?"

"Like someone dropped a Molotov cocktail on my head. I was sure it was gonna kill me, but that wasn't the problem. That would have been a relief."

"Yes, it's pretty unpleasant," Mabel replied. "The biggest challenge with the substance was how to refine it and control the results. The first experiments had…unpredictable consequences."

Carlton laughed. "What happened? Did your researchers break out and roam around the countryside, hunting and gathering their way through the local wildlife?"

"Most of them died horribly. The unrefined infusion was a highly dangerous substance."

"I have to say, I don't think the FDA will approve your drug anytime soon."

"I'm sure you're right. On the other hand, the FDA is never going to find out about it."

"Why did you need to make something like that?" he asked, although he knew the answer. They'd made it because they needed the physical boost it gave them.

"You saw what happened last night," she answered. "Ricardo had the advantage. He would have killed us slowly like he told us he was going to do. Giving you the infusion turned the tables and made it possible for us to survive the night."

"The Society was founded in the 1890s, right?"

She nodded. "Around that time."

"What did you do before you had the infusion? You operated successfully for more than fifty years without it."

"We lost a lot of operatives. This is a dangerous job now, but it was more like a suicide mission back then. We used to give our fighters an edge with other substances, but none of them compared to the primal infusion."

"The caveman infusion."

"If you like. It taps into something from prehistoric times, although people didn't live in caves all the time. You have to understand that a human being is a well of untapped potential. We evolved some incredible abilities in the prehistoric past when supernaturals roamed freely and the world was swarming with dangerous animals. Analysis of prehistoric footprints shows that the average human being of that era was the physical equivalent of a modern Olympic athlete. It was the only way we could have survived to become what we are today."

"Okay, you wanted that for the UUE, and you refined the process as well as you could. That junk is still *rough*, though."

"Learning how to refine it has been a challenge, but now it's mostly under control. As I said, we prefer to do it where we can control the environment. It makes the process much easier for the recruit."

Carlton's stomach rumbled, and he realized he was painfully hungry.

"Huh."

"What is it?" asked Amber. When she turned, she saw that he had his hand on his stomach. "Tummy ache?"

"Didn't you say something about feeling hungry earlier?"

Amber nodded. "We told you you'd need more food, yeah."

"Well, I'm famished." He noticed that his jeans were looser. Not that he'd had a lot of fat to spare, but burning as hot as he had last night seemed to have rapidly melted what little he had. "I feel like I'm fading away back here. Did you ever see that movie where the guy gets cursed, and no matter how much he eats, he just keeps getting thinner? What was that called?"

"It was called *Thinner,*" Amber replied drily.

"Right. Well, either way, I'm starving."

"No worries," Mabel told him. "I figured you'd probably be feeling that way by now. We'll pull off at the next exit and get some food."

It wasn't long before they reached an exit, and Carlton noticed a road sign for a restaurant called The Feed-a-Lot. The lettering on the sign announced, "All you can eat buffet," and Carlton's stomach rumbled again.

"That's where I want to go. The Feed-a-Lot."

"Jesus, Carlton." Amber giggled. "That place is going to make you sick."

"I don't care. It says, 'all you can eat buffet.' I want an all-you-can-eat buffet."

"One all-you-can-eat gorging experience coming right up," Mabel announced, pulling off the highway and following the signs to the Feed-a-Lot.

It wasn't hard to find. The glowing neon sign out front showed a huge, ecstatic-looking hog diving enthusiastically into a trough over-heaped with food.

"I feel embarrassed just walking in here," Amber commented in the parking lot. "I mean, just look at it."

"Amber, dear, be understanding," Mabel chided. "It's been a long time since your first infusion. You've forgotten what it's like."

"If I recall correctly, I went out to a nice French restaurant. This place has a literal hog on it. A very happy hog."

He did look happy. The hog's smile was so huge that it was unnerving.

"I don't care," repeated Carlton. "I want stacks of pancakes. Pancakes and biscuits with Southern gravy, a huge pile of eggs with cheese, a stack of sausages..."

They went inside, and the waiter took Mabel's credit card and told them to "have at it." When they reached the buffet, Carlton piled his first plate high with everything he'd mentioned, plus hash browns and half a grapefruit.

Mabel and Amber turned out to have healthy appetites. Despite her dismissive comments, Amber dug into several plates of pancakes and waffles. Mabel was equally hungry for eggs and fried potatoes.

Neither of them could compare to Carlton in terms of quantity per plate or number of plates consumed. He ate so much that he saw the waiter staring in amazement, then calling a manager for a closer look. The two of them stared at him, increasingly concerned for either his well-being or the profitability of the restaurant.

He thought he should be embarrassed, especially when he noticed it wasn't only the waiter and the manager.

Other people were staring at him too, including a pair of small children pointing him out to their mother.

You know what? I don't care. I'm so hungry I don't care.

As the plates stacked up in front of him and he slowed down, he noticed that Mabel and Amber were staring at him too. They were not only staring but laughing quietly, trying to be discreet but failing.

"What's up?" he asked defensively.

"Oh, it's nothing," Mabel replied. "It just brings back old memories. That's all."

Amber was covering her mouth with her hand. "It reminds me of my first time after receiving the infusion. Let me see. I had a huge stack of *croque monsieur,* several bowls of French onion soup, and a serving of *bœuf bourguignon*. That wasn't all, but I can't remember everything I had. It terrified the staff of the restaurant. What about you, Mabel?"

"Mine was chow mein. That was the popular Chinese food back then. Well, that and chop suey. But I loved the stuff until that day. I had one bowl after another after another. The Cantonese guy who owned the place came out to make sure I was all right. He thought I was about to burst like a balloon. Speaking of which…"

"Oh, yes." Amber gave him a grin that was knowing and mischievous at the same time. "The next part will also be memorable."

Despite their hints, Carlton didn't know what they meant. He was still eating, if slower than he'd been until now. He put a forkful of country-fried chicken in his mouth.

"Memorable how?"

They both laughed, and it hit him. He felt his stomach twist hard, like someone's fist was repeatedly clenching around his intestines. No, like a small animal was trying to eat its way through his stomach to his heart.

"Oh. This isn't good!"

The two ladies laughed hard enough they were having trouble breathing. As for Carlton, he was fighting to keep himself from doubling over. He wanted to get up and run madly for the bathroom, but first he had to get enough control over himself to stand up without an accident.

"You see?" Mabel told him, still trying to control herself. "Your new metabolism can process a lot of food, but it doesn't process it with perfect efficiency. There's a lot of waste, and since your new body does everything harder, stronger, and faster..."

She stopped, leaving Amber to finish the sentence. "Dealing with all that waste is no different."

They laughed again and were still laughing when Carlton finally managed to stand up. Moving as quickly as dignity and tightly clenched butt-cheeks would allow, he made his way to the bathroom.

CHAPTER TWELVE

From Miami to Pennsylvania's Susquehannock State Forest was a drive of approximately twenty hours, but Carlton's eight hours of sleep had knocked a substantial chunk of time off that trip as far as he was concerned.

They had covered a lot of ground before they stopped at the Feed-a-Lot, and now they were moving steadily closer to the headquarters in the wooded hinterlands of Pennsylvania. The countryside was no longer Southern, although it did have a distinctly Appalachian feel as they drove through the western part of the state.

Along the way, they had been forced to move slower to adjust for the changes Carlton was experiencing. Luckily for him, though, they understood those changes, so his off-the-rails metabolism and waste expulsion were nothing new.

As they drove, they developed a comfortable rhythm that managed to prevent anyone from experiencing either embarrassment or frustration. Carlton didn't want to talk about it, and after their juvenile amusement at the situation in the restaurant, the women didn't feel the need to talk about it either.

That explosion of laughter in the restaurant had obscured what was going on between them. No one had been chatty since they left the Feed-a-Lot. Other than small talk about food preferences or music on the radio, the hours had largely passed in silence.

This suited Carlton fine since he was not the chattiest guy. Something told him there was more to it than that. Specifically, he sensed that it had to do with the women in the vehicle being angry at each other.

He could understand that since he was angry too, though it seemed to be hard to hold onto the feeling. Amber had lied to him, and her lies had resulted in the death of someone he would not have wanted to kill.

He didn't know if they could talk that out without him raising his voice, so it was probably better that no one wanted to bring it up. In all likelihood, they both understood that having it out in front of Carlton was not the best plan, but they were both still on edge. The car felt tense, even though they kept their opinions to themselves.

He decided to get the conversation going to break the tension.

"What will it be like when I get there?"

Amber turned to look at him. "Have you ever gone through MEPS?"

He frowned. "MEPS?"

"A Military Entrance Processing Station. You know, where they determine your physical and moral fitness to serve your country."

"No." Carlton shook his head. "I've never been in the military."

"Huh. I'm surprised. You have that look."

Not for the first time, it occurred to Carlton that Amber had probably served in the military.

Mabel spoke up. "Carlton chose a different route when it came to a career. He has the skills we need, just not from military service."

Carlton raised his eyebrows. "Chose? I don't remember choice having much to do with it."

Mabel raised a finger as if to shut him up. "You always have a choice. Even in a prison cell, you have a choice."

"Yeah, but not a very good one."

Mabel shrugged. "A choice is a choice, whether or not it's the one you would have preferred. In any case, when we arrive at headquarters, you will be put through a battery of physical, mental, and emotional tests and examinations. This will be followed by testing to determine your skills in relevant areas.

"Between those, you'll be given doses of truth about the creeps and our efforts to fight them. We like to build a recruit's knowledge bit by bit. Too large a dose too quickly can have negative effects."

"Okay. That would normally have included receiving the infusion?"

"Yes, although obviously, you won't need a second dose. The truth is, I'm not sure how things will go since you received the infusion early, but I *am* sure we will sort it out. Before long, you'll be ready to get into the field."

"Define 'before long.'"

Mabel shrugged. "In the next eighteen months or so?"

"Whoa, hold on," Amber interjected. "I know there's a training process, but that timeline won't work. Can't the Society speed it up?"

"Why?" Mabel asked. "I mean, that's on the fast side."

"We're planning to stage a counteroffensive and reestablish ourselves in Miami, right?"

Mabel nodded. "Once we're ready to, yes."

"We need Carlton if we're going to do that. You said it yourself; he has the skills we need. You can't just sideline him!"

"I don't know about that," Carlton replied, "But for personal reasons, I want to get back to Miami as soon as possible."

Mabel laughed. "Personal reasons, huh? You're just trying to get back to that Chehalis girl, but you're not ready for her yet."

"I'm not ready for her? I can..."

Mabel interrupted. "Uh-uh. Sorry. You're going to have to do as you're told for a little bit. I mean, don't get me wrong; your initiative is appreciated. So are loyalty and obedience."

That last point was made with a sharp look at Amber, who didn't take it quietly.

"Look, Mabel. I did the best thing we could have done under the circumstances, especially considering we were leaving the state. You're still trying to operate according to the old rules. Half-measures and compromises, making bargains with things like Connor..."

"You don't think we should be working with Connor?" Mabel asked, letting her anger show.

Rather than clearing the tension, Carlton had brought it to the surface.

"What *should* we be doing? In your expert opinion?"

Amber cleared her throat. "We should be taking no prisoners. Asserting dominance. Remember, we always have access to the nuclear option."

Carlton perked up, wondering why they were talking about nuclear weapons.

"The nuclear option?" he asked.

"The discussion is over, Amber," Mabel announced.

Amber ignored her. "The nuclear option is letting the world find out the truth about the supernatural. Tearing the veil, we call it."

"Tearing the veil?" Mabel's voice was stern. "Don't you think that would do more harm than good?"

"I know you believe it would," Amber replied. "Maybe it's not that simple."

"What *I* believe? It's what many in the UUE believe, and for good reason. Centuries of experience is not an over-simplification."

Amber was warming to the debate. "Centuries of experience? The UUE is old, but it's not that old. We don't have centuries of experience."

"The human race has *millennia* of experience for the UUE to learn from. How much evidence do you need before you'll take it seriously? I'm telling you, tearing the veil would do more harm than good. There's no reason to doubt that. The world has repeatedly shown that broader knowledge of the supernatural is not handled well."

"There's a context for all those past incidents. A context of ignorance, which is exactly what you're saying we should perpetuate. Yes, people in the past did stupid things when they knew about the supernatural without understanding it. That doesn't mean they would do the same if they understood it."

"Oh, really. Tell me, Amber. In all the witch scares of the sixteenth, seventeenth, and eighteenth centuries, how many *real* witches did they find and execute?"

Amber didn't respond. She merely grew sullen and quiet.

Mabel seemed to feel she had won the debate. "Exactly. None." She looked at the rearview mirror and spoke to Carlton. "When the veil is torn, humanity doesn't respond well. This has been established again and again, and it's part of the reason the UUE exists. The witch hunts are only one of many such examples."

"I guess I can see that," he replied, "but what do you mean?"

He had a vague understanding of what had happened during the witch trials, but most of it was based on having seen *The Crucible* in high school. He suspected the official version of history was not accurate. It rarely was.

"A lot of innocent people get hurt. Herd instinct and self-preservation kick in. In many places, people fight and kill each other over things like skin color, religion, or politics. Add in that the pale kid at the bus stop could be a blood-sucking demon corpse, or the old lady in the spooky house could be a man-eating shape changer, and people get crazy."

"Couldn't they help you wipe out the things you fight? If you had everyone in the world on your side..."

"Didn't you hear what I just said to Amber? People are

not good at spotting the real monsters. They fall back on their prejudices and target the freaky kids and their weird neighbors. Meanwhile, real vampires are good at hiding, and real witches are warded by protective spells. The village witch was likely to trigger a witch hunt during the witch trial era, knowing she was safe because of her wards.

"That's how malicious some people can be. If people knew about the supernatural world, they wouldn't be any help in fighting the monsters that prey on the human race. They'd be more likely to wipe each other out while looking in all the wrong places."

Amber stepped in again. "Nobody's talking about doing it casually without any responsibility. The nuclear option would only be used if things got really bad."

"Okay. What's your other option? If you don't think it's time to go nuclear yet, what do you want to do? Honestly, Amber, it sometimes seems like you want to be radical for the sake of being radical."

"It's like I keep telling you. Zero tolerance. No more deal-making and compromising. No more letting them exist as long as they don't go too far. We wipe them out. Total war until the threat is eliminated."

Mabel shook her head. "You don't see how dangerous that is? You don't think it would have consequences to just start wiping them out as if they wouldn't do everything in their power to survive?"

"*Of course* they'd fight back," Amber replied. "Which would make it that much easier for us to identify and execute them. Listen to yourself, Mabel! It's like you don't want us to win! Do you hate those things or not?"

Mabel didn't answer. For the next few minutes, all she

did was breathe slowly and deeply. It took Carlton a minute to understand what was happening, but then he realized she was fighting to control her anger.

"Yes, I hate those things." When Mabel finally spoke, her voice was calm and self-controlled. "If by *those things* you mean beasts like Ricardo or the necromancer who forced us out of Miami."

Amber was looking out the window, watching the world go by. Her voice was so quiet that Carlton barely heard it. "Well, I hate 'em all."

Mabel shook her head. "They are not all the same. The supernatural isn't evil, Amber. Some of it is dangerous, which is why the UUE exists. The mere fact that something is supernatural doesn't make it the enemy, and even when something is dangerous to human beings, it isn't always the right move to wipe it out. Part of this job is understanding the limits of what we can do and exercising patience when working within those limits."

Amber spun, her voice angry and loud. "Those limits are self-imposed and stupid, and they get people killed!"

Mabel raised her hand, indicating the argument was over as far as she was concerned. "Regardless of what you or anyone else within the organization thinks, those limits are Society policy. If you cannot accept them, you need to spend some time at headquarters for additional training. Perhaps if you were more familiar with how the UUE operates and why…"

"Spare me the condescending bullshit," Amber interrupted.

Mabel lapsed into silence. The argument hadn't

resolved a thing, and Carlton regretted having started the conversation.

For the next half-hour, Amber stared out the window as if she were in a different world, while Mabel stared at the road and drove. The tension in the car was double what it had been before.

Carlton had seen this before, if in a different context. In the CIA, you didn't always agree with what you'd been asked to do. You didn't always understand it.

The thing was, no one ever asked you your opinion. You got your orders, and that was that. If the CIA told you to kill a used car dealer in Antigua, you didn't ask why the CIA wanted to kill them. You just assumed there was a reason for it and got down to business.

Carlton's long experience made him sympathetic to Amber's frustration, though. He could understand it, even if he was shocked by her willingness to confront her supervisor.

One thing he'd always hated about working for the CIA was the feeling you had no control over your own moral choices. That you could be asked to do something evil, and you wouldn't even know it. Or that some limitation imposed from up above might get you killed for no reason.

Who was right? He didn't know, but he was glad he didn't have to decide. He knew what he was doing, and he knew why he was doing it. Confronting the UUE about its strategy was not going to help him achieve his goals.

A short time later, the woods outside their vehicle thickened, with deep patches of dark forest and tall, looming trees. It looked like a park, and Carlton got the sense that they were not far from the Society's secret headquarters.

Amber had not spoken since the argument ended, but she suddenly perked up.

"I could use a restroom break."

Mabel shot her with a paranoid frown. What was she nervous about? They'd stopped to get food or use the bathroom several times, so what was different this time?

Carlton wanted to avoid another argument, so he decided to try to head this one off at the pass. "You know, I could use a rest stop as well. And come to think of it, I'm hungry again."

Mabel nodded. "Very well. If that's how it has to be."

He didn't know what she meant, but the last thing he wanted to do was debate it with her. If Mabel was passive-aggressive, so be it.

They drove on for a little while, then pulled off at a truck stop. After the car was parked, Carlton got out. His arms and his legs were stiff after spending so many hours in the car. After he'd stretched, he walked into the truck stop.

Amber was nowhere to be seen. Carlton went to the men's room and tried not to think about it. His thoughts kept coming back to the spiritualist Amber had tricked him into fighting.

That girl had not been innocent, but was she an immediate threat to the human race? If that was what Amber meant by zero tolerance, he wanted nothing to do with it.

He could still feel the sensation of her neck snapping when the crowbar hit it, and it made him sick.

Maybe Mabel was right. Maybe Amber needed additional training to straighten her perspective out. Coming out of the men's room, he decided to pick up some snacks he knew the women would like, hoping to cool the tension in the car. Amber had mentioned being fond of KitKats, and Mabel had said something about those little mini donuts covered in powdered sugar.

With their mouths full of their favorite treats, it would be harder for either of them to restart the argument. Carlton picked up a Three Musketeers bar and enough KitKats and miniature donuts to keep both women occupied until they reached their destination.

As he headed back to the car with two plastic bags dangling from his fingers, Carlton kept thinking that he could see both sides of the argument. He leaned toward Mabel's side. He didn't think total war was the way to go, especially given how rare it was for war to work out the way it was meant to.

On the other hand, he could remember being on jobs where limitations on the hit had made his life more difficult than it had to be. He'd always found that frustrating like any field operative would, and those were situations in which the worst thing that could happen to you was only death or prison.

As a field operative for the CIA, you took death for granted. It could happen to anyone, and sooner or later, it would happen to everyone. That was one reason most operatives didn't feel bad about taking life. When your own life was on the line as well, it felt like a fair trade.

If anything, prison was more frightening. Still, if you did go to prison, the CIA would get you out via a discreet prisoner exchange. You might be in there for a few years, but it was unlikely to be worse than that.

He'd hated the restrictions that made his life more dangerous in the field, but he'd been able to live with them.

How much more would he hate it if those restrictions didn't only put him in danger of being killed or imprisoned? What if they could result in him being turned into a monster or having his spirit bound to a tortured, rotting corpse?

When he looked at it that way, Amber had a point. In the end, Carlton wasn't sure which side he agreed with, but he decided it was not his business to take sides. He hoped they could make it to headquarters without things getting any worse.

He reached the vehicle and got in the back but didn't notice Amber wasn't there. As for Mabel, she was sitting at the steering wheel and staring straight ahead, not saying anything.

Carlton tossed a jumbo package of KitKats on the front passenger seat, assuming Amber would come back in a minute.

"I got some powdered donuts for you," he told Mabel, but she still didn't speak.

Carlton settled in and unwrapped his Three Musketeers, then took a bite. Amber still did not return.

Carlton was nervous, but he couldn't explain why. He finished his candy bar, and Mabel suddenly heaved a sigh. She put the car in reverse and pulled away.

Carlton realized what must have happened, but he didn't want to admit it. He looked at the truck stop, then at the road ahead of them, then back at the truck stop. As it faded in the distance, Carlton leaned forward and spoke to Mabel.

"Aren't we waiting for Amber?"

She shook her head.

He wasn't satisfied with her answer, but she didn't seem eager to give him more. He sat there for a minute, still leaning forward, uncertain of what to say next, then he decided to go with the obvious question. "Why not?"

"Because she's no longer there. She must have hitched a ride with a trucker or simply walked down the highway while you were in the bathroom."

"How do you know that?"

"It's what I expected would happen. We're almost at the headquarters, so the moment she said she needed a restroom break, I knew she would make a run for it."

Carlton wasn't sure how to feel about that. On the one hand, Amber had manipulated him and caused him to do something he wished to hell he hadn't. On the other, his sense of being part of something was based on having met a handful of people, people he'd expected to go on working with. Perhaps for years.

Instead, two of those people were dead, and one was AWOL. There was no one left from the Miami crew except Mabel and him, and Mabel was the one who'd introduced him to the UUE.

"What are you going to do?" he asked, thinking about how the CIA would have handled a rogue operative.

Mabel was quiet. When she finally answered, her voice was ominous, and the hint of regret in it only made it more so. "I'm going to hope Amber comes to her senses soon.

Otherwise, I'm going to have to do something I don't want to."

As they drove away, Carlton again thought about his years with the CIA and the dim view they took of operatives who walked away without the Agency's permission. He had a sense of what Mabel meant.

Since you ran, Amber, run far and fast. Best of luck to you.

CHAPTER THIRTEEN

It wasn't long before they entered the Susquehannock State Forest. Amber had waited until the last moment to make a run for it, which told Carlton that she had only decided to do it after that final fight with Mabel.

They drove in silence down a dirt road, away from the entrance gates used by campers and vacationers. The opening to their access road was obscured by overhanging pine branches, but Mabel drove slowly through the branches for several feet, after which the path cleared and became the road on which they now were.

At certain points, the dirt road connected with roads that were clearly part of the official park system. When they came to one of those intersections, Mabel slowed to a stop and looked both ways, making sure no one was watching, then drove through.

The Society road was marked by signs that read, DANGER: this road has been closed due to the risk of mudslides. DO NOT ENTER, or something similar.

The entrance to the SUUE headquarters was tucked so

far back in the old woods that it felt like the world had been swallowed by the surrounding trees.

The headquarters was unassuming. A wooden gate across a gravel side road led to a little building that looked like a ranger station. If anyone had driven down the UUE road, they would have come to this station, and a Society employee would have ordered them to turn around and go back.

When they reached the station, Mabel stepped out and flashed her ID at an employee, a woman dressed like a park ranger but not quite. Carlton wondered if her attire was meant to provide plausible deniability. If anyone ever asked about this odd station off a closed road marked by DANGER signs, the park bureaucracy could politely say they had no idea what they were talking about.

The Society ranger waved them on, and they drove around the little building to another gravel road. This one reminded Carlton of a park he'd visited in childhood, where some of the walking trails had struck his youthful mind as impressively dangerous. Like those half-remembered trails, this gravel road dipped into a wooded vale with trees so thick they nearly blocked the sky.

Carlton assumed they were almost there, but the headquarters was buried deep in the vale, where no one would see it. It took them half an hour of creeping slowly down the slope with more of the world being swallowed by the canopy before Carlton glimpsed a fence weaving between the trunks.

The fence was made of heavy close-fitting metal links, rising twelve feet and topped with big spools of razor wire. As deep in the forest as they were, the headquarters was not only hidden but protected by this high fence. If a lost hiker stumbled across it, they would not be able to climb it and cross those razor-wire spools.

If anyone with ill intentions wanted to get in, they would need heavy tools to cut through the thick metal links. The headquarters was a hidden fortress, and although Carlton assumed random people came across it, they had no way of knowing what was beyond that fence.

Outsiders would rarely find it since the trees were so thick as to be virtually impassable, and none of the park's many hiking trails were near it.

Looking around, Carlton realized that hardly any of it would be viewable from the air because of the thick trees on the other side of the fence. It was the perfect place for a secret society's lair.

At last, they came to a gatehouse with thick fencing on either side and a reinforced metal gate. No sign indicated this was the headquarters of the SUUE or gave any clue as to its intended purpose.

Standing at the gatehouse was another man in a Society ranger uniform, the same light green shirt and dark green trousers as a Pennsylvania Park Ranger, but in slightly different shades.

This man checked Mabel's credentials, then raised the gate and waved them through. Carlton was acutely aware that there was no way to escape this facility if you had a mind to. Your only hope would be to get a rope, climb one of the trees to a point above the razor wire, then climb down the rope on the other side without getting stuck.

Even if you did that without getting caught, you'd still

be deep in an almost impenetrable forest with little chance of making it out. Not an impossible task, but close.

Just past the second gate, Carlton saw nothing but more trees. A moment later, though, he saw a series of long, low buildings like sunk-in military constructions. They stretched between the trees on either side, although whether they were housing units or training buildings, he had no idea.

"What are those places?" he asked Mabel. "This is bigger than I expected."

She smiled. "What did you think? That the UUE was five buddies in Miami?"

"No. Well, not exactly."

What he wanted to say was "You didn't seem like buddies". He didn't say that out loud, though. Her Miami operation had been annihilated in the past forty-eight hours, and the last thing he wanted to do was rub it in.

"I know this is all new and overwhelming," she told him, "But never fear. You'll be getting a good look at those places soon. First things first, though. Before you get a closer look at anything else, you need to be introduced and inducted at the Big House."

Carlton expected the Big House to be a large and imposing structure, but its size turned out to be symbolic rather than literal.

The Big House was a cabin not much bigger than the little ranger station at the head of the trail. Mabel parked the car out front and opened the door. "Follow me."

Carlton was expecting it to be bigger on the inside than the outside or something like that, but when they headed in, it was what it looked like from the outside: a one-room cabin almost bare of furnishings, with a fireplace crackling on one wall.

He looked around, confused, but there was nothing in the Big House except a table in the center of the room. On the table was a stack of paper, so Carlton leaned in for a closer look.

He saw the word Charter written in florid calligraphy on the top sheet and discovered it was the original charter of the Society.

It laid out the Society's goals for handling "Unquiet Ephemera" and similar problems, protecting the general public from harmful knowledge of the supernatural, and more along the same lines. There were equally calligraphic signatures at the bottom of the document, the founders of the Society.

Whoever these people had been, they had gone in for the fancy writing. Most of the signatures were so stylized as to be illegible, although Carlton did think he could make out the name Rockefeller among them.

Next to this thick and well-aged document was a small stack of papers bearing other signatures.

"What are these?" he asked.

Mabel pointed at the list of names. "These are all people who have joined the SUUE. That's why we came here first. By adding your name to this list, you agree to abide by the principles and the hierarchy of the Society."

"So, Amber signed this?"

Mabel nodded. "Yes, of course she did. Unfortunately for Amber, she seems to have forgotten what she agreed to when she signed this document. Take all the time you need to read our Charter. I wouldn't want you to make a similar mistake."

Carlton had glanced at it and didn't think there was much sense in reading it in detail. Whatever the Charter said, his real duty was to do whatever his superiors asked him to.

If they wanted him to kill monsters, they'd expect him to kill them. If they wanted him to back off and give the monsters space, they'd expect him to do that. When you looked at it that way, did it matter what the Charter said?

Carlton did think about asking Mabel if he had a choice. Could he still say no? What would happen to him if he did?

When it came down to it, he didn't want to hear another Mabel one-liner about choices and how you always have one even when it seemed like you were trapped. He also didn't want to hear her tell him they'd kill him if he refused.

That was the underlying point behind all her nonsense about choices, wasn't it? Just like the CIA, the Society didn't ask you a question unless they were sure they knew what your answer would be.

Now that the primal infusion was in his veins and he'd seen their secret headquarters, Carlton wasn't sure they would let him live if he said no. He'd passed the initiation and reached the inner sanctum. Surely his only options were to step through or get a bullet in the back of the head and a shallow grave deep in the woods.

It was okay. This was the way to achieve his goals and win a place in Marly's heart and a role in Tully's life. He felt the weight of the wallet while he thought, knowing that taking this step would bind him to the Society and its work.

With a last steadying breath, Carlton mouthed the names "Marly and Tully" before signing the list.

The moment was anticlimactic. He stood there as if waiting for something, then looked up. "What's next?"

When he thought about it later, he realized he'd been half-expecting it to be like the gang. A hidden door would open, and a bunch of thugs would storm in to beat him in officially.

When he'd been beaten into the gang, he could tell that not everyone could take that kind of initiation. The older gangsters might have selected you because they thought you could take it, but that was no guarantee you could.

With the other gang members raining punches and kicks on you, you might lose your cool. You might beg them to stop and remember you were a human being and their friend and neighbor.

If you did that, you were screwed since a coward could not become a member of the gang.

Maybe they weren't going to beat him in. Maybe it was more like the Mafia than a street gang, and they weren't going to hit him. Instead, they'd show him the bullet with his name on it and tell him they were saving it in case he ever betrayed them, or they'd burn a picture of a saint or something.

None of those things happened, though. Mabel saw him look around, heard him ask what was next, and grinned.

"What are you looking for, Carlton? Fireworks?"

"Sorry, it's just that I've been through this before. I was expecting something more dramatic."

"So, what are we talking? Hooded robes and torches? Chanting?"

"A group beating." He laughed at his melodrama.

"Ah. You expected to be jumped in. Interesting that your mind equated the UUE to your gang experience rather than your CIA experience. I suppose it makes sense, considering your past, but the UUE treats you like a professional. That was why you came to our attention. We don't do any of that strongarm stuff."

"You don't? I remember a certain basement in Miami…"

"Okay, there's that." She shrugged. "But that's over. You've been through the worst of it, and you've survived a couple of dicey situations since then too. There isn't anything else we could do to you here that would tell us more than that."

"That's a relief. I mean, I can survive being jumped in. I've done it before, but I'm not eager to do it again."

"Who would be? Listen, Carlton, you're one of us because you chose this work, this life. We plan to trust you. However, there is one last thing we have to do before you go through all the boring stuff."

Here it comes...

"What's that?"

Mabel went over to the fireplace crackling in the back of the room and drew out a glowing orange brand. In the light that shone from the tip of the brand, her face looked demonic, like an evil secret police torturer in a bad movie.

"Goddammit," Carlton cursed. "I should have known it was too good to be true. I should have known I wasn't getting out of this without some hazing bullshit."

Mabel frowned, offended. "Come on now, Carlton. This

isn't what you think." She held up the brand to show him. It was a diamond made of a double intersecting X. "This isn't a hazing ritual."

"Okay, then what is it? That basement full of dead people wasn't hazing either, according to you. What was it you called that? Bonding?"

"More like a prerequisite for bonding. Everyone else has been through something similar, and they wouldn't be sure about someone who hadn't. This isn't bonding either. It isn't a bullshit social ritual. It's a matter of security."

"Really? How exactly will it make you more secure to burn me with a red-hot brand?"

"We have to check you before your membership becomes official. We do this to everyone to make sure those being inducted into the UUE aren't skinchangers, vampires, trolls, or what have you."

"Trolls?" Carlton asked. "Seriously? *Trolls?* Aren't they supposed to turn to stone at sunrise?"

"Somebody has read his Tolkien."

"Huh?"

She waved that away. "Never mind. The point is, we have more than just run-of-the-mill everyday paranormals, Alice, and you will end up down that rabbit hole eventually."

"Okay then. Trolls." Carlton shook his head, marveling at how different the world was from what he'd always been told.

"Anyway," she continued, "the idea is that any clinging specters and spirits will be driven out of you. Some curses and bindings cling on to an operative from their past life, especially if they are unaware of it. We go through this nullification ritual to make sure every new operative starts with a clean slate."

Carlton didn't like the sound of "nullification ritual," but it was too late to worry about that. If this was what he needed to do to join the club, he would do it.

"Okay." He swallowed. "I can do it. Where are you planning to brand me? My arm? My ass?"

"*Property of UUE,* huh?" She laughed. "No, Carlton. Jesus. I'm not going to brand your ass. Traditionally, the brand goes on the chest over the heart, but anywhere on your abdomen is fine." She twirled the brand, smirking. "On the other hand, I could give you the mark as a tramp stamp if you prefer."

Carlton shook his head. "Call me a traditionalist. Right over the heart."

He lifted his shirt and braced himself for the burn.

"Hold on. We've been talking for such a long time that the brand has cooled off. I need to get it hot again to do this properly."

She pushed the tip of the brand into the center of the fireplace, where the coals were glowing so hot it made Carlton's eyes swim to look at them. When the brand was hot enough, Mabel stood and showed him the tip. The double X diamond was glowing fiercely.

"Ready for it?"

"Ready as I'll ever be."

He held his shirt up again, and Mabel went over and pressed the glowing brand to his chest.

The brand didn't burn at first. It felt cold on his skin. In the back of his mind, he remembered having heard something about that. Something about the nerves being destroyed by the burn, so the person being branded didn't feel the heat.

He'd never gone in for torturing his targets as a CIA operative, not even when extra compensation was offered. Others from his former life had talked about it, though. One of them had told him that branding could be almost painless, but the results were unpredictable. He'd never believed the guy, but maybe this proved it was true.

That was when he noticed the burning feeling.

Ah, shit. So much for that.

The heat radiated out from the brand and across his flesh. Had his clothing caught fire? He looked down to make sure, half-expecting to see smoke or flames rising from his shirt. But no, he'd been holding his shirt up away from his chest.

With a sensation somewhere between amazement, horror, and confusion, he saw that there was nothing burning. As the brand pulled away from his skin, he saw only a few faint wisps of smoke.

Those wisps were made by his chest hair as it flash-burned away. There was nothing else. His skin wasn't split or blistered. Hell, it wasn't even red.

Why does everything else hurt so much?

The burning in his chest spread rapidly, burrowing through his body as if he were being eaten alive by an army of fire ants. He opened his mouth to ask Mabel what the hell was going on.

No words came out. It was all he could do to choke out a scream before the burning sensation overwhelmed him, causing him to double over. He ran his hands all over his body, desperately looking for the source of the burning, and couldn't find a thing.

The world upended him slowly, like a building falling over in slow motion before burying a whole neighborhood under falling bricks and broken glass. Carlton fell in a heap, collapsing on the floor as the ants swarmed over him.

He looked at Mabel with desperate eyes. She looked confused.

She's never seen this before. She has no idea what's happening to me.

Her lively eyes were cold and clinical, studying him without concern. She leaned close to him, examining his pupils with scientific curiosity.

"Well, that's new," she commented.

Carlton blacked out.

CHAPTER FOURTEEN

Carlton woke up in a strange place, and his first thought was that he was sick of waking up in strange places. He was on the floor in a dark room. That was all he knew.

Don't they have medical facilities in this place?

He didn't know what he'd expected, but it wasn't this. He should have woken up in the hospital wing, shouldn't he?

At least on an Army cot or something of the sort, but no. He'd woken up alone on the floor in this dark place. He thought it must be a dungeon, but then he saw the shelves along one of the dirt walls, the single lightbulb over a wooden chair, and the wedge-board steps leading to a pair of cellar doors.

I remember this place, or I think I do. Why would I remember it?

Carlton slowly got to his feet, touching his chest to confirm there was no welt or scar from the branding ritual he'd just gone through. There didn't seem to be anything. What the hell was up with the UUE, telling you they weren't going to do any hazing and then branding you on the chest?

He moved over to the shelves for a closer look. Leaning in to see what they contained, he saw a rusted assortment of things that had once been hand tools, along with a collection of cloudy mason jars stuffed with fungus-covered produce of various kinds.

So, this was a cellar. A cellar he remembered for some incomprehensible reason. Had he ever been in this cellar before, with its rusted old tools and repulsive jarred vegetables?

No. He never had. These weren't his memories. He figured out that much before he realized whose memories they were or what had told him they weren't his.

He kept catching flashes of these alien memories. Hands moving jars aside as if looking for something that wasn't there. Hands clawing the dirt floor, feeling the edges of something.

He had a strange feeling he couldn't put his finger on that everything was wrong. Maybe that was it. Maybe he knew these weren't his memories because they didn't feel right, and there was nothing else to it, but whose memories were they?

That wasn't it. The feeling that everything was wrong was there, but it wasn't esoteric intuition. It was simpler than that, and he could hardly believe it had taken him so long to see it.

He knew these weren't his memories because the hands he saw in them were not his.

He tried to move them, but he couldn't. The hands weren't his, so they weren't his to control. He couldn't hold them up in front of him for a closer look, but he focused on them in the darkness. These hands were the hands of a child, a young girl.

Carlton shook his head. "This isn't right."

As he said those words, he heard another voice saying the same thing. "This isn't right."

He did a double-take, then saw that the voice had come from a figure standing next to the chair. Not just any figure; it was the girl spiritualist he had killed. "What the hell? What are you doing here?"

She looked like a normal teenage girl. Not pretty and on the heavy side. Young enough to have not finished growing into the body she was going to have, much less the kind of person she was going to be. There was an ugly too-deep bruise on her neck and she was looking at him, not accusing him of having murdered her but not dodging the unpleasant facts of the situation either.

He stared at her with his jaw hanging open. He'd killed his share of people. Okay, more than his share, considering most people thought it was wrong to kill *anybody,* but none of them had ever appeared to him before.

He didn't know what she was doing here. All he knew was that he wanted nothing to do with it. Whatever this storage cellar was, it was time to get the hell out of here.

The girl stepped in front of the staircase. "I wanted you to see this. To make sure you were paying attention."

Carlton ignored her. Generally, the dead didn't speak to the living. He made an attempt to step around her so he could move toward the stairs and get out of the cellar.

The teen rolled her eyes and heaved an exaggerated sigh while stepping to block him once again. "Like, *really*?"

He looked at her. "What?"

He hadn't expected a dead teenager to talk and act like a teenager.

"*What* what?" she replied, looking directly into his eyes like she thought he was brain-damaged and was watching him closely to see what he got up to.

"Uh, nothing," he answered. "I hadn't expected this. I hadn't expected anything like this."

"You killed me because you thought I was a dangerous witch. A real old-school move, if a little patriarchal. Now you're telling me you didn't think you'd be haunted?"

"Well, when you put it that way…"

"Listen, all right? Just listen up because I've got things to tell you. I need you to hear me out."

"Yeah, okay."

"When you're back to doing whatever it is you're doing now, I'd appreciate it if you could find some way to get me out of here. Seriously, we'll all be much happier when that happens."

"Yeah, that's true." He'd be happier when all this was over. When he wasn't being confronted by the young woman he'd killed. Much happier indeed.

"All right, first things first. What do you think I am?"

"Well, you're dead," he replied. "So, I assume you're a ghost."

She wiggled her hand as if to say "Sorta." "In a manner of speaking, yeah. I'm a ghost. You could also describe me as a spiritual-slash-psychological construct inside you."

She used the words "spiritual-slash-psychological," as if the slash symbol on a keyboard was a word.

"A psychological construct," he repeated to show that he

was listening. He didn't feel qualified to comment on the "spiritual" part.

"Yeah. I'm myself, but I'm also a part of you that grew from your survival instincts. Not so much a personality as a force inside you."

"A force *inside* me?"

He was feeling stupid, like he couldn't keep up with what this girl was telling him.

"Not in *that* way. Ugh, don't be gross. Anyway, I'm able to shape it a little. You follow me? I can make you see things the way I want you to see them. At least, things I've seen."

He looked around the cellar. "So, you're making me see this place?"

"Yes. I'm creating this whole scene. I chose this place because it will help me tell my story."

"What… What's your name?" he asked her.

She barked a laugh. "My name? What does that matter now? It didn't matter when you broke my neck with that goddamn crowbar."

"Sorry about that."

"Yeah, well. That's not going to help me. Anyway, my name is Kimberly Walker."

She pointed at a corner of the basement where the packed dirt floor had been dug up. "I found the old book there."

The ghost of Kimberly Walker, if that was what she was, went on to explain the events that had put her on the path to where their lives intersected. Sometimes she told her story with words, and other times she showed him scenes by shaping the dreamscape.

She gave him little glimpses of memory that felt like ice water splashing on his brain. She wove her story with words and images, making him feel like he had been there.

Kimberly had found the tome she called "the old book." She had no idea how old it was. She'd found it in a senile aunt's basement in Arkansas. When she opened it, she'd realized it was a grimoire.

She taught herself basic spells, although at first, she thought of them as tricks: making objects move, causing a glass of water to freeze, blowing candles out or lighting them, and so on.

It wasn't long before she learned the truth. The spells in the old book were for manipulating the powers of spirits and ghosts. At first, that had frightened her, but soon she began to communicate with them, however rudimentary their communication was.

In truth, having someone, or some*thing*, to talk to was a solace to a lonely girl who had no siblings and never seemed to be able to make friends at her new school. With her mother moving around a lot and her dad never there, she was always the new kid in school.

No one wanted to get to know her. No one ever became her friend, so having the spirits to talk to was wonderful…at first.

By the time she realized the spirits were influencing her, that they were getting more power over her than she wanted, it was too late. She held a banishing ritual and burned the book, hoping that would get rid of the spirits. It didn't stop them.

Kimberly was too smart for her own good. She'd memorized many passages, so the book was inside her.

Burning it wasn't enough to dispose of it or of the spirits attached to it.

The spirits were able to use the memorized spells against her, influencing her as she slept and using her to make mischief and do bad things.

"I knew it was getting worse," she told him. "I couldn't stop it and would never have been able to stop it without outside help. I mean, I wish it could have been otherwise, but by the time you showed up, it no longer could. I'm honestly glad you stopped me from killing anyone."

He'd been listening the whole time, but this last statement caught him by surprise. "You're happy I stopped you?"

She shrugged. "Yeah. I'm not a bad person, you know? I never wanted to hurt anybody, but those things in the old book had a hold on me. I couldn't drive them out, and the only hope I had left was if someone did it for me. So, I don't want you to feel guilty. Not really. I'm at peace with what happened."

Carlton hadn't realized how bad he felt about the killing until she said that. He'd killed so many people that he thought he didn't have any sentimentality to spare for a single person. He had regretted the killing, yes. He wasn't happy about having killed a teenager, someone too young to understand the consequences of their actions. Still, until she said that, Carlton would not have believed he was broken up about it.

When he heard her saying she didn't want him to feel guilty, Carlton felt tears of relief well up in his eyes. He felt at peace. She was telling the truth; he knew that much. Her forgiveness mattered.

"Why do I keep feeling and knowing things from you?" he asked.

"Well, I'm not a hundred percent sure, but as far as I can tell, it happened when I died. It's a hell of a shock, you know? I think it broke me free of the spirit that was attached to me."

"Were you possessed?"

"Not exactly. Possession is when the spirit takes over your body and uses you like a puppet. This spirit was stuck to me like a leech, but it wasn't in complete control. That's called spirit obsession, in case you're interested."

"Obsession rather than possession. Got it."

"Anyway, my spirit clung to you when I broke free of the obsession at my death. I was hanging out there, trying to hide, still not sure what had happened to me, but then you got in a car wreck.

"That kind of…woke me up. I didn't feel like I could let you die."

"I was in danger of dying?"

She rolled her eyes. "What do you think you are, immortal? Hell yeah, you were in danger of dying. Do you have any idea how fast you were going? The shock of the impact was enough to stop your heart."

That's sobering.

"Oh."

"Yeah, 'oh' is right. You were as good as dead, guy. Luckily for you, you had the ghost of a witch girl attached to you. I got your heart to start beating again. Don't ask me how since I don't have the faintest idea. Okay, that's a lie. You were unconscious, so possessing you was easy."

"Wait a minute," he protested, "Just hang on. You're saying you possessed me?"

"Yeah." She shrugged. "I mean, anyone could have done it if they were a ghost with extensive experience as a spiritualist, and you were lying there unconscious."

"Right. But that's... I mean, my free will..."

She blew a raspberry. "Whatever, man. If I hadn't done it, you would have died. So yeah, I revived you, I got your sad little heart beating again, but you wouldn't wake up. I had to plant the idea of waking up and getting the hell out of that car wreck in your head."

"I remember that part. Getting out of the car, I mean."

"I'll bet you don't remember how I was there like a good little angel on your shoulder, whispering '*Live, Carlton! Live!*'"

"Uh, no. No, I don't remember that."

She shrugged again. "Like I said, whatever. It happened, whether you remember it or not. Anyway, that's not the point. The point is the effect it had. I mean, you dragged yourself out of the crashed vehicle, and you know the rest, but the whole experience bonded us. I can't leave. That's the basic problem."

"Okay, I guess you need my help to get out of here? What can I do?"

"It's more complicated than that. You see, that brand they put on you should have destroyed me. That's what it's designed to do: to extract and eliminate foreign spiritual presences. So, you know, my psychic presence inside your spirit is dangerous for me. Should have been fatal. Well, not *fatal*. I mean, I'm dead. It's more like it should have erased me. You can imagine why I'd want to avoid that, yeah?"

"Yeah. That sounds worse than death."

"Dunno since I've never tried it, but I don't wanna find out. Luckily for me, we're bonded on a level where the brand wasn't able to identify me as a foreign entity. Like I said, I'm technically made out of elements of your psychology. Anyway, I was able to shield my specter from the effects of the brand. Unfortunately, that had side effects."

"Like that godawful burning feeling?"

"Yeah, like that," Kim told him. "Followed by total unconsciousness. A coma, really. That's what's going on now. You're in a comatose state, and it's not clear that they'll ever let you wake up."

"What do you mean?" he asked. "Why would that even be an issue?"

"This bunch you run with are real paranoid about dark spirits and witches and all that fun stuff. Anyway, the side effects from the branding have sparked serious concerns in Mabel and her cronies. They're not sure about you all of a sudden."

Carlton had seen how the UUE dealt with those it wasn't sure of. The consequences were standing right in front of him. "Okay, so what do we do?"

"I don't know yet," she answered. "I don't trust these UUE guys. I mean, they sent you after me, no offense."

"None taken." Carlton figured he could tell her later. Right now, he wanted to hear what else she had to say.

"Anyway, I'm worried about what the Society might do. If they get too aggressive in trying to pull me out of you, it might destroy both of us. I'm guessing you want to avoid that, which is why I took the risk of revealing myself to you."

Carlton nodded. "I definitely want to avoid anything that would destroy either of us, never mind both of us. The woman who ordered the attack against you isn't with the UUE anymore. She was…kind of a fanatic. Mabel isn't like that."

"So, we can trust Mabel? Is that what you're saying?"

He shook his head. "I'm not sure. I don't know her well enough to make that kind of assessment. Still, I don't think she'll want to destroy you on sight. She's more reasonable than that."

"What are you suggesting?" she asked him.

"I'm suggesting we tell Mabel. Being straight about it should remove their suspicions."

"I don't know, man."

She backed away. Carlton had no idea what it would mean if she ran out on him. Would she sink further into his subconscious?

"Look," he insisted. "I think she's the best one to help us. I can't make any promises, but that's my opinion."

She stopped backing up. "Okay, on one condition."

"What's that?"

"Those spirits I interacted with through the old book were really fucked up. Damned souls, you know? Their existence was torture; that's why they were so malicious. If I agree to this, you have to promise to do everything in your power to make sure we get separated the right way."

He nodded. "That's fair. What's the right way as far as you're concerned?"

"I want to pass into the hereafter without being

destroyed and without being trapped here as a ghost. I don't want to be like those tortured spirits."

"Okay, you've got a deal. You agree not to interfere when I tell Mabel what's going on, and I agree to use whatever influence I have to make sure they remove you in a way that doesn't destroy you or leave you as a tortured spirit. There's only one problem, Kimberly."

"What's that?"

"I'm not sure how much influence I have. I'm only a novice. They're going to see me as someone who doesn't know what he's doing."

"That did occur to me. I think it's still my best shot, though. They already know something's up. They could escalate to harsh methods anytime they want to."

Carlton noticed she was pressing her fingers against each other in a repeating pattern: thumb to index finger, then thumb to middle finger, then thumb to ring finger, over and over.

She must be feeling anxious. What happens when a witch gets anxious?

"You know," he muttered, "I'm not sure I like the idea of a teenage witch's ghost hanging out inside me."

"Tough shit. You think I like this? Again, gross. We don't have any choice, big guy. We've got to work together."

A ripple passed through the wall in front of him.

Carlton did a double-take. "What the hell was that?"

The walls of the cellar started to vibrate and wobble.

Carlton didn't like that. "Kimberly, what the hell's going on?"

She looked at the shaking walls. "Something's going on out there."

"Out there? Where?"

"In the real world. You know, the world outside your mind? Something's going on."

"What does that mean?"

"It means you're about to wake up. Remember what I told you. I don't blame you for what happened to me. I was trapped anyway, and I'm grateful I didn't end up killing anybody. I do hold you responsible for fixing it now. Do you understand?"

He nodded. "I understand, and I'll keep my promise."

"Okay. Go ahead and wake up."

Carlton blinked several times and opened his eyes to something like the medical facility he'd expected. He was lying on a hospital bed.

That's reassuring, he thought. *They have medical facilities and haven't just dropped me on the floor in a root cellar.*

It wasn't the same as a normal hospital, though. It had the same sterile cleanliness you'd expect in a hospital, but judging by the long, low ceiling, he figured he was probably in one of the buildings he'd seen when they entered the fenced-in area.

Well, Mabel did tell me I'd see what was inside those buildings soon. This might not have been what she had in mind, but...

Kim had told him something was going on, but he couldn't tell what it was at first. There didn't seem to be any doctors nearby. No nurses either. Whatever it was, it would have to wait until he'd cleared his head enough to respond to it.

He tried to stretch his arms and found them stiff but

useable. He stretched his legs, which was painful, but they worked.

Something was holding him back, though. It felt like pressure on his arms and legs, and for the first few seconds, he was too out of it to realize what it must be.

The overhead lights flickered, and he heard gunfire and angry shouts from outside. That was the first time he saw medical professionals, or what he assumed were medical professionals since they were wearing scrubs.

They rushed past him, ignoring his presence as they ran to a weapons locker near the door. As something banged violently on the door outside, one of them entered a combination, opened the door of the locker, and handed weapons to the others.

This was not a situation to sit out, regardless of how he felt. Carlton tried to sit up, intending to run over and grab a weapon. It turned out he couldn't since his arms and legs were strapped to the bed.

The armed medics were taking up combat positions around the room, crouching behind cover and aiming their weapons at the door. Something slammed into the door again, rattling it badly. He didn't think it would hold much longer.

I need to get out of these goddamn straps!

Luckily for him, his CIA training had included a course on escape and evasion, as well as instructions on how to free yourself if you were strapped down. It had seemed like James Bond nonsense at the time, but he was grateful for it now.

Carlton got to work, using the fingers of his right hand

to pull on the strap on his right wrist until he got it loose, then wiggling it until the clasp came loose.

With one hand free, it was a simple matter to free the other hand and then the legs, or it would have been if Carlton had been given enough time. Unfortunately, he had only managed to extract one hand from the straps when the door burst open and a horde of fresh-evants poured in.

CHAPTER FIFTEEN

It was a real test of Carlton's mental discipline to stay focused on freeing himself from the straps while dozens of freshly minted undead ran through the door, howling their lust for human flesh.

He wasn't alone. At first, the rush of undead was held off by disciplined fire. The men and women in scrubs looked like doctors and nurses, but they shot and moved like combat veterans.

Delivering accurate fire from behind cover, they bought Carlton the time he needed to get free. The fresh-evants were distracting, and the strap that held his left arm turned out to be stubbornly tight.

He worked at it while stealing occasional glances at the battle for the door. As long as the defenders maintained their positions without being overrun, they could hold this hospital until the enemy ran out of bodies to throw at them…or until they ran out of ammo.

At first, it worked. A fresh-evant ran through the door,

took a bullet to the head, and collapsed in a heap. Another charged forward with outstretched arms, moaning, and took a shot to the torso.

Carlton thought the thing had been shot through the heart, but it turned out to be a near miss. The creature staggered, snarled, and kept running. The second shot blew its brains out the back of its head, dropping it a few feet from one of the defenders.

So many of the fresh-evants pushed through the door that the defenders couldn't fire quickly enough to take them down. The first human casualty came when four dead things managed to break through, reach one of the defensive positions, and swarm the doctor and the nurse holding it.

The nurse fell back, shooting, but it was too late for the doctor. They fell on him, biting, and blood gushed from his neck.

He gurgled in horror and pain as they ate him alive, but the nurse who'd been holding the position finished him off with a mercy shot as she retreated toward new cover.

As he frantically worked on the left strap, Carlton noticed that some of these creatures looked strange. Stranger than your usual undead corpse, that is.

While many of them appeared to be people who had been grabbed off the street and converted into mindless cannibalistic revenants, some of them had unusual features like pointed ears, extraordinarily high cheekbones, or deeply hooked noses.

These strange features didn't seem to be prosthetics but their body parts, which suggested that not all of the things besieging the hospital were reanimated bodies, or not reanimated *human* bodies.

What were they if they were not human? Based on the way they looked and movies, Carlton could only think of them as goblins or gremlins.

The strap holding his left wrist was as tight as ever, and he was making no progress with it as far as he could tell. More of the undead came in, mobbing and taking down the defenders one by one. Some broke through the lines, saw Carlton lying on the bed, and howled with what sounded like delight.

Well, that's not good.

If he couldn't get this strap off before the revenants got to him, they would eat him alive.

Carlton gave up on the left wrist strap to free his legs, starting with the right.

Luckily the leg straps were not as tight, and he could easily reach the one on the right. As the medics fought to hold the fresh-evants back, he succeeded in getting his right leg free.

The nurse swung her rifle and hit a revenant in the face, knocking it sprawling before it reached him.

Carlton worked the strap on his left leg loose, leaving only his left wrist trapped.

When skill and intelligence fail, brute force remains. Carlton gave up on his attempts to work the wrist strap loose, instead relying on his natural fear of being eaten by ravenous dead people. With desperate strength, he wrenched the rail back and forth until it twisted free, leaving him with a convenient bludgeon.

One of the fresh-evants broke free of the nurse trying

to hold it back, gave an enthusiastic moan, and charged at Carlton with its arms outstretched and mouth gaping.

Carlton had thought of the things as mindless, but the joyful eagerness with which it charged made him question that assumption. He smashed it in the head with the metal arm of the cot and its skull collapsed inward, causing its left eye to fall down its face as it dropped in front of him.

He had just disposed of that one when another one came in at him, this one squealing like a stuck pig. He took another vicious swing and dented the second attacker's skull, causing the squeals to become moans of distress. A second swing finished it off, but then a third and fourth undead thing were on top of him.

It wasn't like his fight with the vampires. He'd only recently had the infusion then, and the primal rage coursing through his body had been out of control. It had felt like it was burning him from the inside out.

Now he could feel the heat, but it no longer burned. Instead, it fueled his will to fight, charged his strikes with tremendous power, and kept him swinging. Every strike was hard enough to cave in a skull, break a shoulder bone, or collapse a rib cage.

He was able to swing the metal arm with full force every time, and he never missed.

That wasn't all. The primal infusion was helping, but these fresh-evants were clumsier than the ones he'd encountered before. They were no less aggressive, but they were less in control of their bodies, making it impossible for them to evade his crushing strikes.

The bodies all looked fresh, or relatively so. However, several of them had bruises or lacerations on their faces, so they had been battered and beaten. Carlton didn't know what the explanation was, but it didn't matter.

His only job was to take them down hard enough that they never got up again. He took down five or six of them with hard blows to the head, then looked around the room to get a sense of what was going on.

The medics had largely dealt with those who had broken through their defensive line, other than the group Carlton had dealt with himself.

Now the battle was concentrated on the door again, so Carlton ran over to help those who were still alive and fighting. He sprinted across the room as a goblin-like thing threw a doctor to the side. Carlton brought the rail down on its shoulder before it could attack him.

The goblin-creature howled in pain, its right arm hanging uselessly. Carlton smashed it on the head, and it moaned and sank to its knees. Blood poured from a massive wound in its left temple, and it wasn't able to recover from it.

Carlton pushed it over, and it fell face-first, never to move again. He jumped toward the door, slashing left and right. For the next few minutes, all he saw was red as the undead fell before him. He went to the open door and got his first glimpse of the battle outside. The headquarters compound had become a warzone, with Society rangers battling packs of fresh-evants everywhere he looked.

A nurse stepped up beside him and stuck a gun against the right side of his face. "We need to secure you. No offense intended." If she pulled the trigger, he'd be dead so quickly he wouldn't have time to wonder what the hell had happened to him.

"No offense intended? I just want to help. I did sign the Society charter, you know."

"Maybe so, but you weren't cleared. Not only that, but you had some anomalies in your purging that we haven't resolved yet."

"So, there were some anomalies. So what? You don't know what that means any better than I do. It doesn't make me your enemy."

He did know what those anomalies were better than anyone else. They were the side effects of having the ghost of Kimberly Walker attached to him. He had no intention of revealing that to anyone other than Mabel. If he did, he might condemn the dead witch to a worse fate than being trapped inside him.

"It doesn't make you our enemy," the nurse replied, "But it doesn't prove you're our friend, either. We don't know enough about you. For all we know, you're the one behind this attack."

Carlton's eyes blazed, but he didn't move. Even with the primal infusion coursing through his veins, he didn't know if he'd be fast enough. Accusing him of working with the enemy, though? That did not make him happy.

"You might want to rethink your position on that," he stated, his voice cold and level.

"Like I said," the nurse replied, "no offense intended."

A doctor stepped forward, shouldering his rifle. "Come on, Nurse. You saw how the undead reacted to him. They were more eager to kill him than anyone else. It doesn't make any sense to think he might be working with them."

Respecting the doctor's authority, the nurse lowered

her gun. She wasn't convinced, however. "We don't know the truth about this man. We cannot trust him."

The doctor shook his head. "I don't agree. Those revenants broke through our lines. If he hadn't stepped in and helped us, we might all be dead. Didn't you see how he moved? That man is infused."

"That only makes him *more* dangerous."

"He's the only infused operative at our position right now. Having an infused operative with us might allow us to stage a counterattack and help our comrades."

"None of you are infused?" Carlton asked.

The doctor shook his head. "Ordinarily, there would be no need for it. You know that Marine Corps saying, 'Every Marine is a rifleman?' Well, it's the same with the UUE. Every member of the Society is trained in combat, but that doesn't mean we're all front-line fighters. Only field operatives receive the infusion. I'm not sure why you received yours early, but I'm happy you did if it will keep us alive."

"It was a field promotion. We had just been in a car crash and were about to be overrun by vampires."

"Sounds like you've had a hell of an introduction to the SUUE."

Carlton shrugged. "I wouldn't know. You're telling me it isn't always like this?"

That cracked them up. "Oh, hell, no," the doctor replied. "This is anything *but* an ordinary day at the office."

The nurse lowered her weapon and stepped forward. "Here, let me get this strap off your wrist. It seemed to be giving you some trouble."

Her voice was reluctant, but she was willing to help now. She reached down to her waist and produced a folding knife, flicked it open with a practiced hand, and sawed through the wrist strap that had given Carlton so much trouble.

When his hand was free, Carlton flexed it to get the circulation going again. "Thanks. No idea why that strap was giving me such a hard time."

"I put that one on," the nurse replied, a tiny hint of a grin on her lips. "You know, as tight as possible."

"Right."

"Here," one of the other nurses told him. "Take this."

He pressed a pistol into Carlton's hand. "It's one thing to beat their heads in, but I feel a lot more comfortable when I can drop them at a distance."

Carlton grinned at him. "I understand. So, what's next?"

The doctor he'd been speaking to pointed across the compound at the Big House. "Based on the fresh-evants massing over there, I'd say some of our people are stuck inside. If we come in from behind, maybe we can break the siege and get them out of there."

Carlton nodded. "Where the hell did all these dead people come from?"

The doctor shrugged. "Doesn't matter, does it?"

"I guess not. Let's do this."

They formed a wedge, then emerged from the hospital bunker with guns blazing. The revenants and their allies were not expecting an attack from that direction.

Carlton didn't know whether they had any strategic sense, but the necromancer who was controlling them probably did. He'd sent more than enough of them to overwhelm the hospital, so a counterattack from the hospital hadn't been accounted for.

As the only infused operative in the attacking group, Carlton was also the only one not assigned a place in the wedge. Instead, he was encouraged to roam freely and take out targets as he saw fit. Holding the twisted, broken bed rail in his left hand and the handgun in his right, he cut a bloody swath through the enemy massing between the hospital and the Big House.

Running across the compound, Carlton shot one fresh-evant in the head from behind, got another one in the neck, and shot a third one through the torso. Unfortunately, only the headshot was fatal, but it didn't matter since he also had that chunk of metal in his left hand.

Every time he pulled the trigger and missed his target, he ran in and finished the creature off with the rail. The primal infusion had given him the strength needed to crush a skull like a Cadbury's Easter Egg, and he was happy to finish the dead things off that way if a bullet didn't do the job for him.

From behind him, the medics moved forward in their wedge, taking carefully chosen shots that almost always hit their marks. Carlton wasn't thinking about their marksmanship, but later, he was impressed with their ability to reliably hit their targets.

A nurse would level his rifle, pull the trigger, and drop a fresh-evant where it stood. On the rare occasion when one of the medics missed, another would fire and finish the job.

Carlton ran ahead, hitting some and missing others. When he missed, his target would turn, its mouth opening. He'd crush its head with the rail, creating a sudden explosion of brains, blood, and bone.

The primal infusion had not made him an elite fighter.

If anything, the combat skills of the doctors and nurses were closer to elite. What the primal infusion *had* given him was the ferocity and striking power of an enraged berserker and the ability to take the fight to the monsters and strike them down in hand-to-hand combat.

Ahead of him, five fresh-evants clustered around a car. He shot one through its open mouth, and it staggered back and fell over. He got another one in the heart, dropping it as it tried to run at him.

Then the other three charged, which didn't worry him as long as he had the rail in his left hand. Unfortunately, it folded in half when he hit the first revenant across the face with it. The thing staggered but didn't fall, so Carlton stuck his gun into its face and pulled the trigger.

The other two were on him, grabbing his arms and opening their mouths. He thrashed wildly to escape, yanking one fresh-evant off its feet and causing it to stumble into the other. They both fell over, and Carlton finished them with two shots as they struggled to get up.

It turned out that they'd been clustered around Mabel's car or, more accurately, the car Mabel had stolen from the vampire. His crowbar was in there, and the rail was as good as useless. Carlton threw open the car door and snatched the crowbar, feeling it thrum in his hand.

The medical wedge came up behind him, looking to him to lead them. Carlton raised his arms in a gesture of triumph and aggression, pistol in one hand and crowbar in the other.

"To the Big House!"

They roared, filled with the joy of battle. Carlton charged, pulling the trigger and swinging the crowbar again and again. His aim was getting better. He shot one fresh-evant in the eye, another in the forehead, and a third in the heart. He was running so fast that he didn't always have time to use the gun, but he liked taking them out with a crowbar better anyway.

A swing from the left brought down one fresh-evant, collapsing the back of its head. A swing from the right took another one in mid-charge, splattering its face all over the grass. A jab with the crowbar's tip knocked another one back, buying the space needed to stick the gun in its face and pull the trigger.

Carlton had always been a fighter. From his gang days to his years working for the CIA, he'd known how to handle violence. He was good at it.

This was different, though. Before the primal infusion, he'd never experienced the wild joy of hand-to-hand combat, the battle madness of a charging warrior. This was beyond a mere fight for survival.

Thanks to the infusion, Carlton was experiencing something transcendent. Then that feeling was gone. He realized that he had pushed too far in his rage and burst through the enemy lines.

He was surrounded by a sea of animated corpses, their eyes both hungry and empty. They didn't seem discouraged by his slaughter. Rather, they seemed more eager, as if they were excited to have more meat.

Most had been human until the necromancer had stolen their bodies with his perverted magic, twisting their deaths for his ends. Some, though, were not human.

Some of the creatures surrounding the Big House were

the ones he thought of as goblins or gremlins, their faces cruel and leering.

Some were massive, undead the size of ogres, their arms bulging and muscular. Their eyes glared fiercely as they moved forward to claim their share of the meat inside the hut.

How much has Mabel not told me?

Carlton was alone and faced with impossible odds.

CHAPTER SIXTEEN

"Come on, then!" he shouted, raising both weapons. "You want some?"

A moment ago, he had been disheartened, his battle frenzy ebbing as he realized how bad his situation was. Now that he accepted his grim reality, it came roaring back. He was ready for anything and everything, and if he fell now, he would fall surrounded by the corpses of his enemies.

He heard the crack-crack-crack of rifle fire from the approaching wedge, and the dead things around him started falling. Ahead of him, the door to the Big House flew open. Mabel leaned out, firing short, targeted bursts with an automatic rifle.

"Come on, Carlton! Run for it!"

He aimed at a dead thing and pulled the trigger, but his weapon was empty. It was down to the crowbar, so he swung that and hit the creature in the head so hard he broke its neck. He kept swinging, knocking over undead one by one.

Ahead of him loomed an ogre, its arms outstretched and its mouth open to reveal yellow fangs. His strike was powered by revulsion and the desire to destroy this disgusting thing that wanted to eat him alive.

As it lunged for him, the crowbar hit it. It staggered back under the impact, not out of the fight, but no longer able to see properly with one of its eyes missing.

Carlton hit it again, knocking out half its teeth. It moaned in distress, although he couldn't tell if it felt pain. He hit it a third time and it dropped. Other creatures grabbed him from behind.

Mabel had switched her rifle from burst fire to single-shot, and she took out one creature behind him with a single well-placed round. A nurse coming up behind him took out another two, and then they were moving again.

"Come on!" Mabel yelled. "*Come on!*"

They ran for the door, the wedge formation falling apart as they crowded through. Carlton stepped inside a moment later, but when the door was closed, he saw that not everyone from the hospital had made it.

Outside, he heard the fresh-evants feeding. They had gotten their hands on fresh meat. The doctor he had spoken to earlier was nowhere to be seen, and Carlton felt sick to his stomach. Those things outside the door must be eating the poor man.

The medical team had taken losses, but they had broken through to the Big House. Carlton looked at Mabel and was shocked when she greeted him with a huge grin.

"Glad to see you're still among the living!" she announced.

"Yeah, you too," he replied, surprised to find he was glad to see her alive. She was not the warmest woman he'd ever known, but she was a comrade, and he was happy to find her here with her gun in hand, still part of the fight.

"Look," he told her, "I know we don't have a lot of time for chit-chat, but I wanted to say you've got a lot to explain."

"Huh? Why's that?"

"I mean, you told me about vampires. You told me about revenants. You didn't tell me there were freaking goblins and ogres!"

"Oh, yeah. Well, there are goblins and ogres. I mean, what can I say? You're going to see some freaky shit in this job. It's one of the perks."

Carlton raised his eyebrows at her. "Perks? You and I have different ideas about what constitutes a tempting compensation package."

"Oh, come on," Mabel replied. "Any job can give you dental, but how many jobs can promise to keep things this interesting?"

Carlton had found the battle outside to be more than interesting, but he didn't want to make that obvious. "To you, this is interesting?"

"Admittedly, this is a tough day at work, but the job is more interesting and less terrifying once you know the basics."

"Trolls aren't covered in the basics?"

"They're in Week Two of onboarding. Jeez, one step at a time. Eager beaver!"

The nurse who had held the gun on him earlier was

looking out through a crack in the door. "The fresh-evants are massing for another attack."

"How long do we have?" Mabel asked.

"No more than a few minutes, and we still need to resolve the issue of the branding."

This again? I just killed two dozen of those things.

"I don't have time to talk about that right now," Mabel replied, all business. "I don't understand what happened with the brand, but Carlton is on our side. Given that we're surrounded by the walking dead, I'll take all the help I can get. That okay with you, Nurse Peebles?"

Nurse Peebles might have had a grudge against Carlton, but she respected the chain of command. Peering out through the crack in the door, she replied, "Yes, ma'am."

Mabel turned back to Carlton. "To finish this fight, we need to get to the necromancer."

"Are you sure he's nearby?"

"To maintain control over this many revenants? Absolutely. He's somewhere close, and this must be straining his ability. It takes a lot of energy to keep this many undead up and going. We might even be able to outlast the bastard. If he runs out of juice, this will get a lot easier."

"Will those things all be dead again?"

"Not right away, no. They won't just fall down, and they won't go away, either. On the other hand, they *will* lose all cohesion if they are no longer under their master's control. Once that happens, they will attack anything, including each other."

"You mean we could just sit in here and relax while those things rip each other limb from limb?"

"They'll rip each other apart, and they'll eat each other.

Basically, it'll be a zombie all-you-can-eat buffet featuring other zombies."

Carlton shuddered. "Don't say that word."

She cocked her head to the side. "What word?"

"You know, the Z word."

Mabel laughed. "Carlton, those things out there are undead. You follow me? Walking corpses. You can call them revenants, or you can call them ghouls, or you can call them zombies." She shrugged. "It doesn't matter what you call them."

"Just don't call them the Z word. It creeps me out."

"Fine. I'll call them the Shambling Corpse Army of the Walking Dead, but I won't call them zombies if it makes you feel better. Either way, we have a choice. We can cut the head off the snake, or we can play the outlast game. Whatever we do, we won't be able to hold this spot for long. If they want to come in here, there are too many of them to stop them all."

"That's a fact." Nurse Peebles looked at Mabel. "We're running low on ammunition. Even if we scored a head hit with every shot, I don't think we have enough in the Big House to take them all. If we don't find that necromancer soon, we're done for."

"It's not as bad as that," one of the Society rangers commented. "We've got extra magazines over here. Take what you need."

Carlton put his eye to the crack in the door to get a look outside. The undead things were crossing the compound from all directions to join the shambling horde in front of the Big House.

"We should do both," he told them.

"Both?" asked Mabel, frowning. "How?"

"I can go out there and look for him. He'll probably be defended, but putting pressure on the necromancer will make it that much harder for him to stay focused and control his undead. Meanwhile, you can move everyone who isn't infused to a more defensible location. Maybe someplace with more ammo than we have here."

Mabel nodded. "That's a solid plan. If you succeed in finding and defeating him, we will cut the head off the snake, but if you don't succeed, we will do our best to wear him out."

Nurse Peebles liked the plan too, if only because it would keep her away from Carlton. "I'll help you move the people, but we need someone to go with this guy."

Carlton shook his head. "I don't need a chaperone. I will go a lot faster if I go alone."

The nurse didn't like that. Even if she didn't want to be around Carlton, she didn't think he could be trusted on his own. She started to open her mouth to protest, but Carlton gave her a little shake of the head to forestall her.

Mabel was nodding. "Okay, Carlton, we've got a plan. Go find a better vantage point, so you can start the hunt for the necromancer. I'll start getting everyone organized to move to one of the intact bunker buildings. When they're ready to go, I'll come out and join you and bring any other infused people I find with me. Once we take out the necromancer, these things should turn on each other. At that point, all we have to do is wait for them to finish each other off."

"How do I get out of here?" he asked. "I mean, we're surrounded."

Nurse Peebles told him, "If you go into the attic, you can loosen enough shingles to get onto the roof. From there, you should be able to see a gap in their lines. If I had to guess, I'd say they're clustered tightly around the door."

Mabel nodded. "That's good. I can come up after you as soon as I have everyone organized down here. Nurse Peebles can lead the breakout attempt."

"Okay. Thanks, Nurse Peebles."

She didn't respond to his thanks. Instead, she pulled the rope to bring down the attic ladder. Carlton thanked her again anyway and headed up.

Forget about her.

He crawled into the roof space, then carefully rose and tested the shingles, prodding carefully. He then put his crowbar to the use it had been designed for.

It didn't take long to lever a few shingles free, and he was fast enough to grab them before they could fall and draw attention from below.

When he'd cleared a big enough hole, he carefully crawled onto the roof. A seething mass of undead had gathered in front of the Big House. They looked like they were getting ready to rush the building.

Stay calm, Carlton. Stay calm.

More were arriving from every corner of the compound. Carlton watched in horror as some came in from the surrounding forest, climbing the fence, then freeing themselves from the razor wire when it snared them.

When Carlton had first seen this place, he'd convinced himself it was impregnable. Now he saw it was vulnerable and in danger of being overrun by revenants, goblins, and ogres.

Whatever else was going on, he needed to stay calm if he wanted to survive. Looking around, Carlton spotted a cinderblock building between two huge nearby trees.

If he could get on top of that building, he could get into one of the nearby trees and see almost everything in the compound. With that kind of vantage point, he had a chance of spotting his quarry and taking the bastard out.

"I hope they're ready down there," he muttered, then leaned over to call into the roof space. "Mabel! We're running out of time!"

In the compound, he saw the undead swarm. When they pressed against the door, their combined body weight would force it open.

Carlton glanced into the roof space and saw Mabel looking at him from the top of the ladder. She hauled herself into the space and crossed to the gap.

"Steady me," she ordered, and he helped her onto the roof.

"All right," she told him. "I'm ready to roll."

Carlton looked into the roof space but didn't see anyone else. "I thought you said you were getting... Oh! We're the only infused ones here, aren't we?"

Mabel nodded. "Yeah, I'm afraid so. Recruitment has been down, and we've got a lot of territories to cover. If we survive this, I'll launch a much more intensive recruitment effort in the coming quarter."

Carlton frowned. "*If* we survive this? Not having second thoughts, are you?"

Mabel pulled around the combat rifle she had slung. "Not at all. Just waiting for you to get a move on."

Below them in the Big House, the medical staff and rangers started their sortie. Guns blazed at the front door, and revenants fell in all directions. Organized into a tight formation, the escape force began to fight their way to a more defensible location.

The counterattack was enough to ensure the enemy's attention didn't stray to the roof.

"Looks like they're focused on the others," Carlton commented. "Let's go for it. Target is that cinderblock building between those trees over there. We get up on the roof, into the trees, and look around for the necromancer."

"All right," Mabel replied. "Go."

Carlton ran across the roof, dropped to the ground, and rolled onto his feet. Mabel was right behind him. They ran for the cinderblock building, reveling in the power and speed of their infused bodies.

Mabel grinned beside him. "Feels good, doesn't it?"

"Yeah," replied Carlton. "Yeah, it does."

Their lives were in more danger than they had ever been, but they enjoyed the feeling. The primal infusion had burned when Mabel had given it to him, but now pure ecstasy pumped through his veins. They ran across the compound side by side.

Ahead of them, revenants dropped down from the top of the fence and headed awkwardly in their direction.

"Looks like we've got a fight ahead of us," Carlton noted.

"What else is new? Let's run over 'em."

"Couldn't agree with you more."

The revenants ran at them, arms outstretched and mouths gaping. A horrible moaning sound came from their throats, like wind blowing through an empty building.

Carlton didn't slow down, just raised his crowbar for a killing blow. The energy of the primal infusion surged through him, making him feel more alive than ever.

You know, he thought, *I'm really starting to like this job.*

CHAPTER SEVENTEEN

As Carlton closed on the charging revenants, more of the creatures spotted the two humans running across the compound and homed in on them.

As much as he hated referring to them as zombies, Carlton couldn't help thinking of the two basic types of zombie movie.

In old-school zombie movies, the undead were slow. They shambled along, and an agile person could run circles around them. The main danger was their numbers. Although they were easy to avoid, a thousand slow zombies could block every avenue of escape.

In the newer zombie movies, the undead were fast. They could run as swiftly as a healthy adult, so it no longer mattered if they outnumbered you. One fast zombie was a major problem.

These things were not from a slow zombie movie. No, these were fast zombies. A little less spooky but far worse when it came to fighting.

Must be the difference between fresh-evants and regular revenants.

That was all the time he had for thinking as a bunch of fast revenants closed on them. Carlton swung his crowbar at the first and hit its outstretched arms so hard he shattered the left elbow, spinning it to face away from him. When he hit it, it moaned in surprise, an oddly comical noise for a zombie to make.

Not a zombie! A revenant.

Mabel fired several times, and the closest revenants dropped one after the other. The one Carlton had hit in the arms was still facing away when the bullet hit, shutting off its limited mental functions like turning off a lamp.

Another one came in fast. The middle-aged woman had a huge wound on her face, and she looked like someone had been eating her when she'd transformed.

Based on her shrieks as she attacked, she took the whole thing personally. She came in so fast Carlton had to sidestep, aiming his strike at the back of her head as she went by.

The crowbar dropped her, sending a big gout of blood from her mouth. Before he could check to see if she was down, another revenant grabbed his arm.

Carlton caved in the creature's head, then took out the two behind it with well-aimed crowbar slashes. Mabel fired steadily, dropping one revenant after another. Ahead of them was the door of the cinderblock building. They were almost there.

"Come on!" Mabel yelled. "Let's get inside!"

Between the two of them, they had managed to clear a path, so they ran for the front door. Carlton got there first and held it open for Mabel. He let go when she got there, and she slammed it shut seconds before the revenants caught up with them and threw the deadbolt for good measure.

"That ought to buy us a little time. You know, I understand that it's fun to get up close and personal, but it would have been quicker to use your handgun."

"Yeah, about that. I'm out of ammo."

"Jesus. They had extra ammo at the Big House. You should have grabbed some."

"I got distracted."

"Well, there's a weapons locker here. There's a weapons locker in every building. Just reload quickly."

She walked over to the wall and entered a combo on a keypad. A door swung open, revealing a selection of rifles and handguns, along with loaded magazines.

Selecting the type of ammo he needed, Carlton grabbed three magazines, then replaced the empty one.

If there was a weapons locker in every building, the UUE must have expected an attack might happen. There had been a weapons locker at the safe house in Miami too, even if that one had been emptied by the greedy priest.

Carlton wondered if this had happened before or if this was a disaster the Society had prepared for, even though no one had yet dared challenge them directly.

When he was reloaded and ready for anything, Carlton looked around. They were in a garage, with a selection of vehicles in various stages of repair or modification.

Nearby was a heavy Land Rover, modified so it could move over rough terrain even better. He wondered what it would be like to drive a vehicle capable of handling almost any terrain on Earth.

Mabel saw him staring at it and sighed. "Maybe when you grow up, I'll give you a chance to play with the big boy toys. Right now, we need to get up on the roof before the undead come inside."

The front door shook under a heavy impact, then shook again. Something outside was trying hard to get in, and it wouldn't be long before it knocked the front door off its hinges. The undead would soon be pouring in after them.

"Right." He turned to Mabel. "How do we get up there?"

"Through that hatch."

She pointed at the ceiling, where a metal hatch gave access to the roof. Carlton headed for the walkway leading to the hatch. After he'd made it up, he slid the bar aside to open it, then pulled himself onto the roof.

"All right!" he called down. "Come on up!"

Mabel was halfway through the hatch when the front door came off its hinges and clattered heavily to the floor. Revenants poured through the opening, their mouths open in anticipation, moaning with delight at the thought of tasting human flesh.

"Jesus, Carlton! Pull me up!" Mabel yelled.

He grabbed her by the arms, hauled her through the hatch, and slammed it shut as the undead reached the bottom of the walkway stairs.

"Are they capable of opening that hatch?"

"Not right away. Let's get up those trees."

"Hold on. I think it has a lock."

He was right; the hatch could be locked from the

outside. The lock was rusty with disuse but looked serviceable. Putting it in place would make it much harder for the undead to reach them. The rusted metal stuck, but he pounded it with his hand several times, slamming the lock into place with all his strength.

When he stood, Mabel was climbing one of the two trees. Carlton ran over to the other one, pulled himself onto a low-hanging branch, and kept climbing until he had a clear view of the compound.

"Find the necromancer!" she called. "He's down there somewhere!"

"Yeah, yeah," he muttered. "It was *my* idea."

It wasn't easy with all the undead moving about. He wondered how the hell the necromancer had put together an army like this.

Hundreds of people must have been killed to stage an attack of this size on the Society headquarters. When Mabel had taken him to that basement for his initiation experience, she'd obviously had no idea she was declaring outright war.

They didn't know who their enemy was, but he had made it his personal mission to erase the UUE from the face of the Earth.

The survival of the Society depended on Carlton's ability to spot his hiding place, but how? There was no black-robed figure down there, glowing with unholy light while he used the powers of Hell to control his undead army.

All he could see was the army itself, a random assortment of undead humans and other things, which he didn't understand enough to know if they were undead.

He hadn't received any training from the Society yet, so he fell back on what he knew. Based on his experience with the CIA, he decided to evaluate what little he knew about the necromancer, then use that knowledge to find him.

The man was obviously obsessed with dead things.

Why else would anyone become a necromancer?

He was obsessed with dead things and bringing things back from the dead.

Why would someone be obsessed with bringing things back from the dead?

Because he was obsessed with the fear of death.

What did that imply?

For all his messing about with death, a necromancer must have an abnormally high fear of dying. His involvement with necromancy probably began as an urge to overcome and conquer death. Even if he was being reckless by waging war on the UUE, he would try to keep himself safe and away from danger.

He looked for a place where the undead were grouping away from the main group. That might be where the necromancer was hiding. He wouldn't leave himself without bodyguards, and he wouldn't stand out in the open, where he'd be easily spotted.

He'd probably present a moving target to avoid easy detection.

Carlton could do this. He now knew what to look for.

There was a large gathering of revenants and other creatures by another building, but that was likely the spot where the rangers and medics had made their stand. That wasn't where the necromancer would be. There was too much personal risk there.

There was another knot of revenants by a tree, but they were besieging an unfortunate ranger who had gotten stuck up it alone. He had run out of ammo and was using his rifle as a club to knock them down as they clawed their way up to him. Carlton wished the man luck but couldn't spare any time for him.

There. A knot of revenants slowly moved together at the edge of the battlefield, not focused on attacking any humans. There wasn't any reason for them to cluster unless they were guarding something. The question was, were they guarding the necromancer?

Carlton studied them carefully and saw what he was looking for. He glimpsed a pale hooded sweatshirt deep in the middle of the revenants.

He wasn't sure it was the same sweatshirt he'd seen on the necromancer in Miami, but it seemed unlikely to be a different evil sorcerer.

"Mabel!" he shouted. "There!"

She looked in his direction, and he pointed at the clump of revenants among which he'd spotted the sweatshirt. She shaded her eyes with her left hand to get a closer look, then gave him the thumbs-up.

"I see him, Carlton! Good work!"

She held up her rifle and sighted down the barrel. This wouldn't be an easy shot without a scope, and so it would take her a minute to set up.

It wasn't clear they had a minute. The hatch on the roof below them flew open. The rusted lock had given way, and it spun through the air to drop to the ground below.

A revenant clambered through the hatch. It moaned with excitement when it got its eyes on Mabel.

Fresh meat. That was all these things care about.

The dead were so eager to get through the hatch they crawled over each other, pulling each other down as they tried to get through. That delayed them, but three of them made it onto the roof, struggling to stand and groaning in hunger.

"You've got to take the shot, Mabel! I don't know if I can hold them!"

"Well, you'd goddamn better hold them! I need to wait for the right moment!"

She was right, but these things could climb, and if they succeeded in reaching her tree, it wouldn't be long before they sank their teeth into her legs.

Carlton repositioned on his branch, looking for an angle from which he could take them out one by one. He only had a pistol, and he wasn't sure he could make the shots from this distance.

He'd learned these creatures wouldn't give them a second chance. If he missed one, it would be eating her before he could take another shot.

Even a first chance was far from guaranteed. One of the revenants saw him, and it ran across the roof, hands held wide, mouth gaping like a black hole.

As it reached the branch he'd used to haul himself up, Carlton aimed at its head and pulled the trigger. It lost its grip on the branch, tumbled off the side of the building, and disappeared.

Carlton pulled the trigger and hit a revenant in the torso. He didn't kill the thing, but he managed to make it lose its footing and fall as it grabbed at the branch Mabel was on.

Mabel looked so calm and self-controlled on her branch that Carlton knew she must be slowing her breathing, lining up the shot while entering the sniper's semi-meditative state of mind.

She only needed a few more seconds, and he could give her that. It was just a matter of shooting the revenants as they climbed the tree to get at her. The only trouble with that was they had only two weak points. If he didn't hit his target in the head or the heart, it was anybody's guess if they'd react.

He hit one in the head, and it fell the way it was supposed to. He hit another in the chest, and it lost its grip but started climbing again a moment later. He fired a second shot into its heart, and it dropped like a shot bird plummeting to earth.

He was about to shoot a third when he had to deal with a revenant climbing after him. He shot the thing in the face and it tumbled away, but before he returned to Mabel, she took her shot.

As she pulled the trigger, one of the revenants grabbed her leg. Carlton blasted the thing, but the harm had been done. When he looked at the necromancer, Mabel had hit the shoulder and not the head.

The necromancer was wounded but not dead. He went down, grabbing his wound, and disappeared behind his guards.

Was it enough? Could the necromancer's spell be broken by a wound?

At first, it looked like the answer was yes. All over the compound, the effect was visible. A revenant walked into another revenant as if it didn't see it. Two revenants bumped into a third and reacted viciously to the contact, clawing its face like they were trying to rip it off until it realized what was going on and fought back with equal fury.

The wave of chaos passed rapidly through the undead army as the creatures bumped stupidly into each other, knocked each other over, walked blindly over each other, or turned on each other with cannibalistic hunger.

Not all of them crashed into and clawed at each other. The necromancer's enchantment retained its hold over nearly half of them. Those remained focused on bashing their way through doors or windows or climbing trees. They'd succeeded in weakening the spell, but they had not broken it.

On the roof below them, two of the ghouls were rolling around, trying to bite each other's throats out. One stepped off the roof. Another one did the same thing a moment later. Yet another tried to climb the tree after Carlton, while two more clambered onto Mabel's branch.

He had to deal with the one coming after him first. He had no other choice. Otherwise, it would take a bite out of him before he would get another chance to stop it.

Its pale hand wrapped around the branch he was sitting on, and a moment later, its eager face appeared, moaning excitedly.

One thing about revenants. They're always happy to see you.

Carlton shot the thing in the head, which made its eagerness evaporate along with its brains. As it did, Carlton heard a branch snap and spun in time to see Mabel fall, battling a clutching revenant as she dropped.

"Mabel!" he shouted.

She could have died when she hit the ground, but he'd seen her shrug off a high-speed car crash like it was a fender-bender. She didn't die when she landed, but the revenant did. Its head hit a rock and split open, leaving a wet red stain on the gray stone.

Mabel lay stunned on top of it. The horrible thing had cushioned her fall, but her problems were far from over.

The undead closed on her from all directions. They might be fighting each other, but fresh meat was fresh meat.

To those that saw her on the ground, no other sight was as appealing. They wanted to rip her to pieces and cram their bellies full of her flesh. To Carlton's amazement, Mabel was still conscious. As the revenants closed in, she struggled to her feet.

If she was alive, he would have to save her.

He could do that. With a ferocious roar, he jumped out of the tree, shooting as he dropped and holding his crowbar at the ready.

CHAPTER EIGHTEEN

In retrospect, diving from the branch was the stupidest thing he had ever done.

He had seen a man killed by a shorter fall than that. He had seen another man crippled, both of his legs breaking in a dozen places.

He didn't think about that. The only thing he thought about was saving Mabel from the revenants, and the infusion's primal power had taken over.

He fired as he fell. To his amazement, the first bullet went through a revenant's head, causing the thing to fall face-first to the ground.

When he landed, he bent his knees to absorb the shock and experienced a weird moment.

I'm unhurt. I just jumped out of a tall tree, and I'm unhurt.

The moment passed, and he swung his crowbar into the teeth of an onrushing revenant. He spun back toward Mabel and blew away the one leaning over her. He spun again and slashed at another revenant, then shot two more, one through the chest and another through the head.

Revenants, unlike people, did not get scared. They didn't become demoralized, no matter how many of them were killed. They just kept coming, as motivated at the end of a long day as they had been at the beginning.

This was a huge advantage over an army of the living. On the other hand, the living didn't turn on each other when their commander was shot.

Mabel had been stunned by the fall, but she quickly recovered. "Holy hell, Carlton. Talk about an epic rescue."

They stood back-to-back, scanning the area for fresh attackers. None appeared, and the revenants in their immediate vicinity that were still under the necromancer's control were destroyed.

"Look," she said, pointing.

All over the compound, revenants were grappling each other or biting each other, or bashing at each other with clumsy fists.

"They're turning on each other now. The necromancer must be losing control."

Carlton had no idea why the undead were so violent, but it seemed to be true of all of them. Under the control of a necromancer, they could be turned against a specific target, but without the necromancer's power, they tried to kill anything that moved.

"Do you think he's dead?" Carlton asked.

Mabel shook her head. "I don't think so. Not yet. We've got to find him."

She didn't suggest going back up the tree, and Carlton didn't blame her. Falling from that height with a revenant clinging to her back must have been traumatic.

They moved across the compound back-to-back so

nothing could surprise them. When they crossed between the buildings, most of the revenants were too focused on destroying each other to notice them.

For a handful of the creatures, that was not the case. When one of these exceptions saw them, it howled and ran in their direction. When that happened, Mabel gunned the thing down.

Once or twice, the creature was too close for her to aim. Carlton used his crowbar, bashing it down.

When they were a few hundred feet away from the garage, Carlton caught a glimpse of a small group moving away from the battle in a cohesive unit.

It was the only cohesive unit left, which could only mean one thing.

"There." Carlton pointed, and Mabel nodded.

They moved closer and saw the necromancer limping and clutching his bloodied shoulder. He was surrounded by undead bodyguards. They were the only revenants he still had control over.

They moved around him in a loose, vaguely defensive formation as he tried to make his escape, shuffling along as if they didn't know how to play such a passive role. To a revenant, it makes much more sense to run howling at your enemy and eat his flesh while he screams, not make an orderly retreat while protecting your commanding officer.

"Where are they going?" Carlton asked.

"There!"

She pointed, and Carlton saw that a large gap had been torn in the perimeter fence. This must be where the attack had started. He wouldn't have believed it, but they had infiltrated through the thick forest just beyond the fence. If they got into those woods again, he might never find them.

"Come on!" he told Mabel. "We've got to catch them!"

He took off without thinking to make sure she was keeping up. After a few steps, he glanced behind, not feeling her presence at his side.

She was dragging her left leg behind her, clenching her teeth. Sweat stood out on her forehead.

When he looked at her, she stopped. "I can't do it."

"Shit! I wasn't thinking."

She'd fallen off a building just minutes ago.

He was so used to thinking of her as invincible that it hadn't occurred to him that she might be injured.

Her voice was raw and ragged. "I'll heal quickly. Just not quite yet."

The necromancer was making for the breach in the fence almost as slowly as they were, but they wouldn't catch him unless Carlton went by himself.

"I'll go alone," he volunteered.

She shook her head. "You're still a rookie. A hell of a fighter, but still a rookie. If you go on your own, he's going to kill you."

Carlton looked at the tear in the fence. "That breach is really big. Wouldn't the Land Rover fit through there?"

Her eyes went big. "Yes. You're a genius! You'll have to carry me back to the garage."

"I'm on it!"

He ran back and scooped her up, then carried her to the cinderblock building. All around them, revenants continued grappling and tearing at each other. Most of them didn't even look in their direction, but one or two noticed them as they ran by and moaned with hunger.

When they reached the cinderblock door, two revenants interested in the prospect of fresh meat broke away from the others and moved in their direction.

"We don't have time to deal with those two," Mabel told him. "Get inside."

They went inside but discovered they were not alone. A revenant was bashing another revenant's head into the floor as they entered, but it dropped its defeated foe and turned to look at them, making a sound like, "Aaaaah."

"I don't think so," Carlton replied, setting Mabel on her feet and firming his grip on the crowbar.

The revenant stood and repeated the sound. "Aaaaah."

"Well, if you insist." Carlton smashed the thing's head, splattering its brains on the floor. It looked at him for a moment, then tumbled to the floor.

"Get into the Land Rover!" Mabel told him. "They're coming!"

He glanced through the open door. The two curious revenants were almost on them. Mabel threw open the Land Rover's driver's side door, so he clambered into the passenger seat as she hit the remote control for the garage doors.

Carlton locked his door as the two revenants ran in, heading for the Land Rover. One of them slammed into his window, its eyes huge and impossibly eager, drool pouring from its open mouth.

Mabel hit the gas, and the Land Rover shot through the garage door as it opened, tearing off the bottom half in a spray of splinters.

They bounced wildly across the yard, not stopping for anything in their way. When their path was blocked by a knot of fighting revenants, they smashed into them, splattering them in all directions.

As they approached the gap in the fence, Carlton was no longer sure they would fit. Mabel didn't share his uncertainty. She floored it as they got closer, causing the Land Rover to fly through the breach and making Carlton gasp in shock.

The trees were packed so close to the fence that he expected them to go straight into one, but Mabel drove skillfully. She yanked the steering wheel to the right and dodged the first tree, then yanked it left and dodged the second tree. Then the necromancer was ahead of them.

His screen of revenants had crumbled to almost nothing as he lost control. When they caught up with him, most of his bodyguards were mindlessly tearing at each other. Two still limped beside him, moaning mournfully.

The Land Rover hit a pair of the creatures that was attempting to rip each other's eyes out. One of the bodies was torn in half, and the top flew into the trees with its mouth still open and snapping at the world. The other one was pulled under the tires and flattened.

There was a patch of new growth ahead of them, thicker than the surrounding trees. The Land Rover wouldn't get through a grove that thick, and the necromancer knew it. He dove into the trees and disappeared from sight.

"Fuck! He's getting away!"

Carlton unlocked the passenger door and threw it open after Mabel slowed enough to avoid him dying on impact.

"Carlton, wait!" she warned, but it was too late.

He leaped out and rolled, coming to his feet among the thick trunks.

The necromancer was just out of sight. Carlton couldn't hear anything over the roar of the Land Rover's engine, but he saw branches moving ahead.

The vehicle roared, and Mabel tore off in another direction. Carlton had no idea where she was going. He was on his own for now. It was up to him to stop the necromancer from getting away.

He took off, but the ground fell away into a steep ravine after a few feet. Carlton was moving so fast he almost tumbled in, but there were so many trees that he was able to catch one and stop his descent before he built up too much momentum.

There was a streambank below, and the necromancer was almost there. If Carlton wanted to catch up, he wasn't going to do it by carefully picking his way down. Trusting the trees and the undergrowth to slow his descent, Carlton hurled himself down the side of the ravine.

It was halfway between a jog and a fall, with bits that could be described as a tumble. Carlton made a point of sticking his arms out to catch tree trunks now and then to keep from going end over end the whole way down.

When he reached the bottom, the necromancer was running along the streambank. The wizard was alone. In the trees behind him, Carlton could hear the last two revenants snarling and snapping at each other like mad dogs.

The necromancer's wound had weakened him enough that he no longer controlled any of the undead. All he wanted to do was get away. Carlton knew that if he lost sight of the man again, he would disappear.

"I'm coming for you!" he yelled, and the necromancer glanced back.

He got a glimpse of terrified, desperate eyes. Then the man was stumbling away, one hand clasped over his wound.

Despite everything he'd done in the past few hours, the primal infusion was still strong. He should be exhausted, but energy surged through him. He took off along the stream bank, gaining on the necromancer so rapidly that he could hear the man repeating, "No! No!"

There was a muddy bank along the side of the stream, and the necromancer glanced up, his eyes filled with desperation. Grabbing an overhanging branch, he tried to run up the bank, hoping to disappear into the trees.

He took a step into the mud in front of him, but when he tried to lift his foot for another step, he couldn't pull it out. As Carlton closed, he tried to extract his other foot. That one came out halfway but wouldn't come any farther. He fell forward, holding himself up with an overhanging branch.

The necromancer was trapped and twisted in the most awkward position imaginable. He was unable to either escape or defend himself.

"By the River Styx, *NO!*" he cried.

Carlton stopped a few feet from him. "I don't think your spirits are listening."

The man glared at him. "I asked too much of them. If I had been more patient, you'd be dead."

Carlton was surprised to see he was no older than his late twenties.

"You know, a necromancer ought to be at least forty years old," he told the man.

The man sneered. "What do you know of the Black Art? I have no choice but to surrender to you, but do not mock something beyond your ability to understand."

"Surrender? Who said I was going to let you surrender? You killed a lot of good people back there."

"Good people? I don't think so. In any case, I was only trying to get vengeance for my dishonored master. He was a great man, a mighty necromancer, and you destroyed him when I was *so close* to bringing him back from the Gray Lands. You not only killed my dream of reviving the greatest master of the Black Arts this land has ever known, but you also burned any hope of unlocking the mysteries he'd intended to pass down. The UUE is a pestilence."

Carlton thought about the burning grimoire and the strangely preserved and pieced-together corpse that had lain on the bench next to the ledger in the basement in which he'd been initiated into the Society.

"Wait, are you talking about that twisted old body you were trying to put together from spare parts and decorate like a gross craft project?"

"Those weren't spare parts, you imbecile! Those were my master's limbs!"

"Okay, Renfield, if you say so. How did you track us to that church after we left the basement?"

The necromancer was still angry, but he was happy to talk, if only as an alternative to being killed on the spot.

"I was nearby when you attacked my sanctuary, but I

needed time to put an appropriate response together. So, I cast a tracking spell. Cornering you at the chapel was well within reach of my abilities. When you survived that attack, I faced a greater challenge. I followed you to this general area, but the tracking spell failed, and I needed time to build my army.

"I knew what to do, though. Once I realized your headquarters was in the state forest, I examined the maps until I found an area remote enough to contain a compound like this. Imagine my delight when I came to scout the area and saw a mysterious fence topped with razor wire."

"Yeah, in retrospect, that was a dead giveaway. How did you collect all those dead bodies, though?"

The young man grinned unpleasantly. "For a master of the dead, that wasn't challenging. If you watch the local news, that question should answer itself."

Carlton didn't know if a train had derailed or an airplane had plummeted from the sky or what, but he did know this smug man standing in the mud before him was a mass murderer. It was time to make sure he'd never do the same thing to anyone else.

"Well, I've got you dead to rights." He pulled the handgun out of his belt with his left hand. "How about we finish this?"

"That isn't necessary, is it? I am no longer a threat, and your Society would surely benefit from having access to a highly skilled necromancer for research purposes."

"I don't know. I'm just a rookie. I can't tell if you're highly skilled."

The necromancer scowled. *He* thought he was among the greatest of all time, a potential rival to his dead master's abilities. He tried to change the scowl into a sickly smile. "No, you're right. I'm a mere nobody, and I throw myself on your tender mercies."

Carlton noticed almost too late that the man was pressing the fingers of his left hand together in an intricate and repetitive pattern. "You're casting a spell, aren't you? Goddammit!"

He raised his gun and pulled the trigger, but the necromancer had raised his hand. His gun only had one round left, and that round disappeared in a flash of black fire as it came out of the barrel.

Something happened to the gun, too. Carlton felt a change of texture he couldn't describe. When he looked down at it, the gun had turned black. A breeze blew in from the trees, and the gun collapsed into dust and blew away.

Fuck it. Let's do this the hard way.

Most people would have been horrified by the necromancer's games and stood there staring at where their weapon had been and the spiraling clouds of particles disappearing in the breeze. Not Carlton.

He swung the crowbar, and the necromancer let go of the branch and threw out his arm to block it. The arm shattered on impact, and the necromancer fell with a cry. Mud splattered his face, covering his eyes in thick black stickiness.

He was still working the fingers on his left hand, trying to use his magic, and that magic was indeed powerful since he had succeeded in transforming Carlton's gun to dust in his hand.

Carlton raised the crowbar, and the black fire flashed

again. He was already swinging, but when he saw that dark light, he expected the crowbar to collapse into nothing before it hit the necromancer. Instead, the tool-turned-weapon flashed with a pale and spectral light before snapping the man's neck.

The crowbar had absorbed the attack spell and neutralized it, and then kept going. It was clearly much more than a hunk of metal.

The necromancer lay in the mud, twisted in humiliation, beaten and broken and dead. Carlton stared at him, not wondering who he was or what had driven him to this strange death. Not wondering anything.

The Land Rover came up the stream bed. Mabel must have driven to an access point and followed the stream up to find him. It had been a good idea, but the job was done. She hadn't thought he was ready to face the necromancer alone, but she'd been wrong.

The necromancer hadn't killed him the way she'd predicted. He'd killed the necromancer the same way he'd killed vampires and revenants and who knows what else.

The Land Rover's door flew open, and Mabel jumped out and ran over. She peered over Carlton's shoulder at the necromancer's shattered remains.

"Jesus, Carlton, the crowbar? You really like to do things the hard way."

That was enough to snap him out of his daze. He grinned at her. "Not the hard way. The Carlton way."

"Help me get this mess in the back of the Land Rover. We did it. The battle is over. Now there's nothing left but the cleanup."

CHAPTER NINETEEN

Carlton told Mabel what had happened before the Land Rover pulled into the compound. Mabel turned off the motor and looked at the destruction. The surviving Society rangers, medics, and other members had already started the cleanup.

For the most part, the undead had destroyed themselves after the necromancer lost control of them. They lay in clumps all over the compound, still tangled up with hands in each other's hair and fists buried in each other's heads or bodies.

The revenants' urge to commit violence had been overwhelming. When they were no longer directed by the enchantment, they had turned on the nearest moving thing and ripped it to pieces.

Most had killed each other more or less simultaneously, but a handful were still twitching and attempting to stand on ruined legs so they could go find another victim.

Their focus on homicide was mindless and complete. They glared at everything they saw around them, struggling to get broken legs under them or drag themselves across the compound when they couldn't walk. Their jaws were still snapping, their eyes still filled with malign fury.

Misery sure as hell loves company, thought Carlton. *All these things want to do is stop everything else from moving.*

The Society's fighters had come out of their bunkers and were going around the compound and methodically shooting revenants in the head whether they were moving or not. One of them would give a revenant the finishing shot, then another would grab it by the ankles and pull it away, to be added to a growing pile of the dead.

It was a macabre scene, especially when you considered all these things had once been living beings, no better but no worse than anyone else.

"What are we going to do with all these bodies?" Carlton asked.

"That's being taken care of," Mabel told him. "The relevant authorities have been informed, and they're making arrangements to return the bodies to their families for burial. There'll be a believable explanation for every death. Let's get out there and lend a hand."

They got out of the Land Rover and helped with the cleanup and returning things to order for the next several hours. Carlton didn't know if anything like this had happened before, but he assumed this was one of the biggest battles in the history of the Society. Headquarters had taken severe damage that could not be fixed in a single day.

Mabel sent a team to place a temporary barricade over the tear in the fence and another team to search its length for more holes. She also ordered the recall of as many operatives and agents as could be spared to headquarters to provide extra security while everything was being put in order. Her official title had been Agent in Charge of Miami, but Mabel was clearly a force to be reckoned with in the Society.

While this was going on, a detachment of recruitment supervisors and medical staff came looking for her. They were led by Nurse Peebles, who had emerged from the battle with no serious wounds. As far as he could tell, Nurse Peebles hadn't trusted him for a second, but he was happy to see that she had made it…until she started talking.

"Now that the battle's over, we need to decide what to do about this guy."

She nodded in Carlton's direction, unwilling to say his name.

"What to do about him?" Mabel raised her eyebrows. "Is there some concern I'm not aware of?"

The others looked at Nurse Peebles, who was clearly the spokesperson. She drew herself up and looked Mabel straight in the eyes. "He didn't pass the branding. There's something corrupt about him. That could be the reason for what happened here today."

Mabel shook her head. "What happened here today? I'll tell you what happened. A necromancer died some time ago in Miami, and his apprentice became obsessed with bringing him back from the dead to complete his course of instruction. He was an unusually talented apprentice. During Carlton's induction, we unknowingly destroyed his master's body and the ledger he was using as a grimoire. That ruined the apprentice's plans, which made him angry, so he used a tracking spell to follow us and unleashed an attack we weren't expecting. Our Miami operation was virtually wiped out, but that wasn't enough for him. He followed us here and engineered a mass casualty incident to get the bodies he needed to stage this attack. Carlton had nothing to do with it other than helping me destroy the master necromancer's body, and he had no idea he was doing that."

Nurse Peebles took all this in, but she wasn't so easily convinced. "Even if you're right that he had nothing to do with this attack, he failed his branding."

"No, he didn't." Mabel's voice was hard. She was clearly accustomed to this sort of confrontation. "Something strange happened at his branding, yes, but that doesn't mean he failed. As far as I am concerned, Carlton is a full-blown operative. If not for my reluctance to flout convention, I'd make him an agent right now. Didn't any of you see what he did today? You're looking at the man who killed the necromancer in single combat. He won us this battle!"

Nurse Peebles had lost, and she knew it. Her supporters drifted away, and those who remained looked at their feet or glanced at her nervously.

"Very well." She nodded. "I'll accept him as one of us, but we still need to determine what happened at his branding."

"That will be my immediate priority," Mabel told her. Nurse Peebles walked away without saying any more.

"You know," Carlton remarked in a joking tone, "I'd be happy to flout convention."

Mabel glanced at him. "What's that, Carlton?"

"I'm just saying that I'd be happy to start a new tradition of honoring hard work with promotions to full agent. Seems like an excellent policy to me."

She grinned. "Don't push it."

Carlton burst out laughing. "All right, but what does your training program have to offer that this experience hasn't given me?"

She shrugged. "You improvised effectively today, but not everything's about improvisation. You still have a lot to learn about the different creeps out there in the world, the best ways to dispose of each when necessary, and how to negotiate when that's possible. Like I said, don't push it. You have more than enough time to learn now that we're no longer on the run or under siege."

He shrugged. "I'm not in any rush. A few months of class time might be a welcome change of pace after the past few days."

"I hear that. Now, why don't you go help the others clean up all these dead bodies? You can make sure all the undead are dead again. That tends to be obvious, but it pays to check. You don't wanna get bitten by one of those things."

Carlton was about to ask her whether being bitten by the undead could turn you into one of them but decided not to bother. He was about to start his training, and he was sure they'd cover that.

His real introduction to his coworkers came over the next few hours as they methodically cleaned up the compound.

Carlton's job was to give each of the undead a fatal rap on the head with his crowbar just in case, after which a pair of coworkers would grab it by wrists and ankles and haul it to the growing mountain of bodies. He found that many of his coworkers were not so bad, despite being a little awkward to talk to initially.

First, they cleared the open areas of the compound. Then they searched the buildings one by one, going from room to room to remove dead bodies and rescue survivors. Fighting for multiple hours was exhausting work, and cleaning up after such a fight was even more exhausting. As they went, his comrades drifted to their bunks one by one, too exhausted to continue.

Thanks to the infusion, Carlton didn't flag, no matter how many hours went by. He worked into the night and was still there when the flatbed truck arrived to remove the dead from the compound. He helped the drivers load the bodies into the back to eventually be returned to their loved ones.

It was hard work, but it was a pleasure to do it, despite the revulsion of handling the messily dead. The primal infusion made hard physical work uniquely satisfying, and he was far from having enough of it.

The door of the Big House opened, and Mabel came out. She watched him loading the dead under the moon and stars before finally speaking. "Take a break."

He dropped a body into the truck and turned to her. "Yeah?"

"I wanted to thank you for everything. You've really stepped up, and I'm not just talking about saving my life, although that's part of it. We've never had a new recruit who did so much so soon."

Carlton put his hands in his pockets. "I'm sensing a *but*."

She looked him in the eyes. "I know something is going on. Nurse Peebles wasn't right about you, but she *was* right about one thing. Something happened with the branding."

Shit. This wasn't good. It was one thing for Nurse Peebles not to trust him. She was a hard woman, and he didn't hold it against her. However, Mabel was his sponsor. She had seen something in him and picked him for the Society.

Carlton's every instinct told him to try to hide it. Inside his head, he heard the nervous voice of Kimberly Walker. "Are you sure, Carlton? Can we really trust her?"

Carlton took a deep, steadying breath, squared his shoulders, and started talking. "I do have something to tell you, but I need you to listen to the whole thing before you make any decisions."

She gazed at him for a moment, then nodded. "Okay. I'll hear you out."

"That spiritualist Amber killed in Miami? Amber didn't kill her; it was me. Amber manipulated me into going into that building. She said she saw someone grabbing a kid and going in there. I had no idea what we were really doing. When we got inside, she assigned me to the downstairs while she took the upstairs, but then the girl and her spirits ambushed her. When I came upstairs, I found the spirits swarming all over her. The girl ran at me, and I swung the crowbar in self-defense. I killed her, but her spirit didn't go away. It attached to me instead."

"You're telling me you came into the headquarters of the Society with the ghost of a teenage witch attached to you?"

"I didn't know," Carlton protested, "But that's what she

told me when I was out. She was able to hide deep inside me so she wouldn't be destroyed by the brand, but now she can't get out. She wants my help to get out of my body without being destroyed."

"She talks to you directly?"

"Yes. I was talking to her when I was in that coma, just before the necromancer attacked."

Mabel stood thinking. The trees surrounding the compound swayed in the night breeze. Carlton was struck by how peaceful it was, given how little time had passed since the bloody battle that had raged in this small space.

When Mabel spoke, her voice was calm and measured. "Carlton, what happened to that girl was not your fault. You had only just joined the organization, and Amber was supposed to guide you through a relatively simple task. She wasn't supposed to go to that house, and she didn't have permission to kill anyone. She manipulated you."

"Yes, I know. I don't blame myself, but…"

"It was your hand that held the weapon."

He nodded. "Yes, and that's why I will do everything in my power to help Kimberly move on safely. She made a mistake, yes, but she doesn't deserve to be erased from existence for it."

Mabel ran a hand through her hair and sighed. "The truth is, this problem is not that easy to resolve. I have to admit that I'm not sure how to handle it."

Carlton frowned. "What's the problem?"

Mabel waved the question away. "It's too much to go into right now. Let's just say there are technical issues. Issues I don't know the answer to, but I will look into them."

"Is that a promise, Mabel? I'm not comfortable having a ghost attached to me."

"That's a promise. I will look into it and try to figure out what can be done."

She was silent, and Carlton got uncomfortable. There was one obvious question she hadn't mentioned, and he didn't want to end this conversation without clearing it up.

"What about me?"

"What about you?" she asked. "The ghost isn't trying to hurt you, is she?"

"No." He shook his head. "I mean, Nurse Peebles wasn't the only one who questioned my right to enter the Society after what happened at my branding. There seems to be a widespread opinion that I'm tainted. The people who thought that didn't know the true story. Now that you know, what does this do for my hopes of joining the SUUE?"

"Oh, that." Mabel paused for a beat, and Carlton held his breath, surprised by his reaction.

Was he *that* eager to join the Society? He'd been roped into it, for all Mabel had to say about choice. Why did it matter so much to him?

"You know," she replied, "the skeptics aren't going to change their minds anytime soon. If you couldn't change their attitudes by killing the necromancer single-handedly, nothing you do will matter to them for a while. It could well be that only time will convince them. Some people will call me stupid for trusting you, but they can't stop me from doing it."

"So, this doesn't change anything?"

She shook her head. "No, this doesn't change anything.

I'm going to see to it that you become an operative. You're good under pressure, and we need that in the UUE. I won't listen to anyone who tries to tell me otherwise."

"Thank you for your trust, Mabel. You won't regret it."

She chuckled. "Let's see if you still feel like thanking me after you've gone through the training. Some of it is…intense."

"I've been meaning to ask you about that since you gave me a field promotion earlier today."

"I did, yes. I declared you a full operative of the Society, and as far as I'm concerned, you earned it. That doesn't mean you don't need more training since you definitely do. You've still got a lot to learn, and learning what you need to know might help you with your ghost problem. I'm counting on it."

"Why?"

"Because it will take a lot of research to find out if there is any way to solve your problem without destroying the ghost. It's basically fused with you psychologically, so there's also the question of whether we can remove it without hurting you. Resolving these questions might take longer than you would prefer. If that's the case, knowing everything you can about ghosts and ghostly phenomena should help you live with the situation until we can resolve it."

"Okay. I can see that."

He heard Kimberly say, *Great. So, you and I are long-term roommates?*

Maybe so, he replied, *but we're working on it, Kimberly. Mabel promised us.*

Gross. Just gross.

"Besides," Mabel commented with a sardonic grin, "whatever oddities you have, I'm not in a position to throw stones."

"What do you mean?" he asked, but she shook her head. She wasn't interested in talking about it now.

"Okay," he replied. "You don't have to tell me. I'm grateful for the opportunity, Mabel. I won't let you down."

She was a strange woman. She could be humorous and warm, but there was an underlying coldness that came out at odd moments. It came out now; her voice was hard-edged and pitiless.

"That's good since I'm making a choice. I'm taking a risk with you. Some people think that's foolish. If my choice is proved to be as foolish as some people believe, I promise you I will make another choice."

He didn't love being threatened, but the possibility that your employer would kill you was implicit in both gang membership and employment by the CIA.

This is nothing I'm not used to.

"Another choice? What does that mean?" His voice was level, not worried.

"I will leave no stone unturned until I bury you."

He shrugged. "That's understood."

She laughed. "I guess that's the benefit of recruiting ex-CIA."

"I guess so. If the exit interview involves a bullet to the back of the head, it takes a special kind of man to sign up for the job."

"Sorry if I offended you."

"No. Like I said, it's just the way things are in this type of job."

"True, but I do have a tendency to be…cold. I don't know if Amber told you, but I've been with the Society for a long time."

Carlton nodded. "Yeah, she told me. She also told me only newbies were interested in your backstory."

"That's probably true. You see a lot of weird things in the Society, and I'm not that weird when it comes down to it. Still, my long history with the Society gives me a level of influence that not every agent has. Unfortunately, it also gives me a lot of baggage."

He wasn't sure why she was in a sharing mood, but since this might be his only opportunity to get solid information, he played along.

"Everyone has baggage, especially in my line of work."

"I'm sure that's true. Anyway, I'm sorry for being cold sometimes. It's just that I have to fix my mistakes, and while I rarely make them, it still hurts. I've had to do it once or twice."

She hadn't told him much. Carlton had the feeling that Mabel was an all-time expert at not giving away more than she had to. As she spoke, her eyes were unfocused, staring at some unnamed memory from her past.

There was a long and awkward silence. Carlton still wasn't sure about her. Was she really sharing anything, or was this an emotional manipulation tactic?

If the boss was sometimes warm with you and sometimes as cold as a block of ice, what were you supposed to do with that? She wanted him to think it was just a manifestation of her past trauma, her regret for having to hunt down "mistakes" who had betrayed the Society.

At the same time, she wanted him to know beyond the

shadow of a doubt that she would hunt him down without hesitation if he failed her. It would be easier to deal with if she hadn't shared her regrets.

Whether it was a sincere expression of emotion or a tactical maneuver, Mabel snapped out of it. "Hurry up and finish so you can get some rest, okay?"

"Yeah, sure. Let me ask you one thing, though."

"Go ahead."

"How long do you expect training to last?"

"I want you to get your training done quicker than normal, so you'll be on an accelerated program. I'm thinking it will probably be close to six months."

"Six months? That's not so bad." It seemed that Mabel had listened to Amber on this point. He wouldn't be going through the full training program before he went to work for the Society.

"You'll test out of a lot of the required classes," Mabel went on. "I'll recommend that you be accelerated. You have the perfect first target."

Carlton frowned. A target already? "Who?"

Mabel smiled in response, but the coldness was not directed at him. "You said that necromancer was trying to avenge his master, right?"

He nodded. "That's what he told me. We destroyed the greatest necromantic master of the twenty-first century or some such nonsense. Never knew that burning an old notebook could have such dramatic consequences."

"Well, the necromancer isn't the only one who believes in revenge."

CHAPTER TWENTY

Miami was quiet in the hours after dawn. The doors to the nightclubs were closed. The dance beats were silent. The party people had gone home to sleep it off.

More importantly for Carlton and Mabel, all the vampires in the city were fast asleep. The two were crouched on the roof of a parking garage six months after the attack on the SUUE headquarters in Pennsylvania.

Carlton had completed the Society's accelerated training course. He'd learned about the supernatural world, although mostly from the perspective of a hunter learning about his prey.

He'd learned about the strengths and weaknesses of revenants and vampires, what set a fresh-evant apart from everyday revenants, how to out-think a troll (not the most challenging course), how to counter typical goblin ambush tactics, and many similar topics.

At last, he officially graduated, and Mabel had asked him if he wanted to take a road trip.

"Where are we going?"

"Same place we came from. It's time for our counter-offensive."

Now they were sitting across from the building where Ricardo was hiding.

"He's in the basement," Mabel told him. "Or that's what Connor says."

"Where is he? Didn't you say he was going to meet us here?"

"Oh ye of little faith."

Carlton wheeled and saw the shirtless, leather-jacket-wearing rock star-type who had irritated him so badly six months ago.

"Connor." Carlton nodded. "You've healed nicely."

The last time he'd seen Connor, the man had been spread-eagled on the hood of Ricardo's car after an extended torture session. He wouldn't have expected the man to recover quickly from that sort of treatment.

Connor shrugged, a smug little grin on his face. "What goes around comes around, as Ricardo is about to find out. It's like Mabel said; he's nesting in the basement. Why don't you head on over there and pay him a visit?"

"Details first," replied Mabel. "I want to know what I'm dealing with."

"Details? What details?"

"What happened when we left? Carlton almost killed Ricardo, but it looks like he managed to get control of Miami anyway."

"Ah. That part is probably down to Carlton too. He took out that necromancer, yes?"

Carlton frowned. "Where did you hear that?"

"Easy, Carlton. Connor hears everything in time. That's

why we do what we can to maintain a good relationship with him."

Connor bowed slightly.

"As I was saying, no one could stand against the necromancer. He had serious power, even if he was reckless about using it. If you two hadn't pissed him off, Ricardo would have been no match for him, but the man was so obsessed with getting his revenge on you that he followed you to Pennsylvania. The rest, as they say, is history. In any case, Ricardo has not been a stable overlord. He's been on edge since he came back to Miami."

"I imagine so," replied Mabel. "Carlton practically beat him to death with a crowbar. That would make anyone edgy."

"Quite. He came back to the city with serious damage to his body. Serious enough that it took time to heal and left him vulnerable for a few nights. That was a time of chaos. You'd just pulled out of Miami, and it was a real free for all. It's ironic, really. With the UUE here, all the strange things in the city could live and thrive, more or less. With the UUE gone, we almost wiped each other out. If you slept in the wrong place, you might never wake up. Ricardo had to hide in the sewers like a rat and nurse his injuries."

"I see. When did he show his face again?"

"A few days later, but half of us were dead by then. All the young blood. Everyone who could have given Ricardo a run for his money. They'd hunted and slaughtered each other like pigs. All he had to do was to step out of the shadows, announce that he was here to restore order to Miami, and most of the strange things of the city were happy to follow him."

"Most, but not all?"

He nodded. "Most, but not all. I would never follow him, for one thing. I owed him a debt. But there were still a handful of the young ones left, and the strongest and cruelest at that. While I skulked in dark places and did my best to stay alive, he gave the others a choice. The few who resisted him were hunted down and disposed of. Since then, Ricardo has worked to consolidate his power. I haven't dared show my face except to the few who owed me favors, but I never stopped looking for my opportunity."

"Revenge?" asked Carlton. "For what he did to you?"

"Revenge, yes, but also freedom. Until Ricardo is dead, I walk the streets in fear. You don't think I'll tolerate that forever, do you?"

His eyes glittered as he spoke, and Carlton realized what a dangerous enemy Connor could be.

"In any case," Connor continued, "finding this opportunity took some time. Ricardo did not forget the lessons of the chaos days. He never rests in the same spot for more than one day. It's a paranoid practice, but it's protected him from those who seek to destroy him. Up until today."

Mabel spoke up. "I contacted Connor to let him know we were coming to town. He'd managed to find out the identity of one of Ricardo's human servants and was watching him to find out where Ricardo slept. When he had an answer for me, he gave me this address, and here we are."

"Doesn't it make you nervous to put the finger on him?" Carlton asked. "I mean, he hurt you pretty bad last time."

"You don't strike me as a literary man," replied Connor, "but perhaps you have heard of Captain Ahab?"

"Captain Ahab? *Moby Dick*? Sure."

"I would strike the sun if it insulted me." There was that gleam in Connor's eyes again.

"I see. Well, we'll take care of your little Ricardo problem. Don't worry about that."

Connor chuckled. "Ah, the UUE! You people have so much self-confidence! I was expecting you to arrive with a hit squad. Instead, there are fewer of you now than the last time I saw you. Are you sure you can complete this task?"

Carlton turned to Mabel for guidance. He still didn't have an assigned team or an agent to work under. Ever since he'd left the headquarters in Pennsylvania, it had just been him and Mabel.

"We're a two-person crew for now," Mabel confirmed. "But I think that's ideal for a soft opening like this one. Miami has been a rogue city for half a year. We're going to change that, and we're going to do so in such a way that no one will ever question our claim to this city again."

Connor raised his eyebrows. "I am beginning to wonder what I've gotten myself into. The events of the past several months have not taught you humility, I see."

"When did humility protect anyone from the creeps of this world? Humanity is safe when the creeps know we have it in our power to utterly destroy them anytime we choose to do so. They've forgotten that in Miami, but they're about to be reminded."

"We shall see. My interest in this matter is to see Ricardo punished for what he did to me. And by punished, I mean reduced to dust. I've made no commitment to the

UUE as far as your other projects are concerned. You'll have to make those work on your own."

Mabel nodded. "I assume our old deal is still in place, though?"

Connor nodded. "I'll continue to share information with you from time to time, yes. Mabel, there were those who put a lot of hope in that young necromancer. Some believed the UUE would finally be broken by his rampage. The sheer ambition of it! I'm told he derailed an AMTRAK train to get the bodies for his army of revenants."

Mabel laughed. "If you're going to kill a king, you'd better not miss. The UUE is about to remind Miami's creeps of that."

"Yes, I believe you are. But the creeps, as you call them, have recovered from the chaos days. They've built up their numbers, and they've learned to love their freedom. With Ricardo gone, assuming you succeed in killing him, there is every possibility that the chaos time will come again. I might believe that the UUE is a stabilizing force, that it makes the supernatural world work more smoothly by removing the Ricardos from it, but to most of the city's creeps, you are oppressors."

"What's your point, Connor?" Carlton asked, his voice challenging. "Maybe it's time we started oppressing them."

Mabel gave him a warning look. He could see the worry that he would end up like Amber on her face.

Connor just smiled. "Miami is still a wild place. I do hope the UUE will be a stabilizing force, but you have a lot of work to do. Best of luck to you both."

Mabel only smiled. "Do you hear that, Carlton? You have your work cut out for you." She turned back to

Connor. "You can expect to hear more from Carlton and his team."

Carlton didn't know what to make of that. *Carlton and his team?*

Connor took it in stride, though. "Fair enough." He turned and stepped off the roof of the parking garage.

Carlton's heart skipped a beat. He didn't like the man, but no one wanted to watch a suicide happen. He rushed to the edge and looked down to see Connor plummeting toward the street. He expected to see him hit the sidewalk and burst open like a balloon, but the man transformed into a crow and flapped away.

"He likes to do that," Mabel told him. "He's a drama queen."

"I thought he was killing himself!"

"Why, because you're always a jerk to him?" Her voice was filled with laughter.

"Uh, I guess not. He doesn't care what I think."

"You're right. He doesn't."

"Wizard?" Carlton asked.

They'd told him in one of his training courses that some wizards could shapeshift, becoming whichever animal they'd established a relationship with.

"Skinchanger," Mabel answered. "There's usually a light show when wizards pull that shit."

Carlton wasn't sure if she was joking or if she was revealing more of what was behind the veil.

"I'm still getting used to all this," he muttered.

"Understood. You ready to go?"

He nodded. "How hard can it be? They're just Ricardo's human servants, right?"

"Well, yes and no. They're human, but a vampire like Ricardo isn't going to hire a bunch of chumps to guard his body while he's sleeping. These men are killers, and they're highly motivated. Typically, a vampire's servants are not just working for money. Sometimes they hoped to be turned if they served their master well. Sometimes it's a religious thing."

That seemed strange to him. "A religious thing?"

"Yeah, like, 'The master commands and I obey.' Real Hollywood stuff."

"Right." As far as he could tell, she was talking about Hollywood in the 1930s. "But this is Miami. They've probably been snorting coke all night, in which case they'll be asleep right now. Let's do this."

"I wouldn't count on it, Carlton. But yes, let's do this."

They descended to street level, then checked to make sure no one was watching before they crossed the street to the front door. The building was long abandoned and boarded up. Carlton knew that didn't mean anything.

On the front door was a notice from the city, stating that the building had been condemned. Carlton knocked loudly on the door three times. There was no response, so he knocked even louder.

"City inspection crew, open up! We know you're in there! Squatters are not permitted!"

There was still no response.

Mabel spoke up. "If we have to come back, we're coming back with the police!"

A lock rattled, and the door opened. It only opened a crack, and a bloodshot eye peered out at them. "Yes?"

Carlton couldn't shake the feeling that he was talking to

Renfield, Dracula's crazy servant. He was thinking of the movie from the nineties where Renfield had been played by Tom Waits.

"City inspection crew," he answered. "You need to let us in."

The eye stared at them for a few seconds, then the man blinked and cleared his throat. "ID card?"

"Of course," replied Mabel smoothly, flashing a card at him.

"Hmm. I guess it's unavoidable."

That seemed like an odd response, but the door opened, the man stepping aside as it did so. When they entered, he'd be behind them, which didn't seem ideal.

"Let me go first," Carlton started, but it was too late. Mabel was already moving. She went in, but Carlton held back.

The man stuck his head back out. "Coming in?"

It was now or never. Carlton slammed his shoulder into the door, knocking the man into the wall behind him. A gun fell from his hands and clattered on the floor, and Carlton slammed the door shut as he passed through.

There was no need for anyone else to see what was about to happen.

The man looked at him with wild, desperate eyes, and Carlton wondered if Connor had given them a bad address. This guy didn't look like a vampire's servant. He was a balding, middle-aged man, more furtive than predatory.

Then he started yelling.

"Protect the Master! Protect the Master! Kill the intruders!"

So much for that. Carlton kicked the man in the jaw,

knocking him unconscious. A gun barked from the other side of the room, and a hole appeared in the wall to the right of his head.

He spun to the left to see Mabel take a gunfighting stance and pull the trigger.

BAM, BAM, BAM.

A man slumped to the floor, still clutching his gun.

Someone else glanced in from the hallway and aimed a gun at Mabel. Carlton shot him in the head, and blood splattered the wall behind him.

They were in a living room with a TV that looked too old to work and a coffee table with a bottle of water on it. Someone had been eating a platter of raw hamburger. Blood was pooled under the ground beef on the plate.

Other than the two dead men and the unconscious one, there didn't seem to be anyone else in the building, but they needed to be sure.

"We've got to clear the building," Mabel told him.

"I'm on it, but what about this one?"

Mabel glanced at the unconscious man on the floor. "That guy doesn't deserve to live, but I don't want to kill him in cold blood. Zip-tie him for now."

Carlton reached down to his belt and retrieved his zip-ties, then cuffed the man to a hot water pipe. His eyes fluttered open, and he snarled at Carlton.

"You stay away from the Master! Stay away from him, or I'll kill you!"

"Is there anyone else in here?" Carlton asked him.

His face got crafty. "Many of us are here. We are Legion. You understand?"

"Uh-huh." He turned to Mabel. "Let's clear the place."

They went from room to room like soldiers on a counterinsurgency mission or cops raiding a suspect's house. Their prisoner kept shouting the whole time, mostly stuff about the Master.

The Master was going to drink their blood. The Master was going to gut them like sheep. He would eat not just their bodies but their souls. They would learn to love him the way he had, but it was too late for them.

"The more I listen to that guy, the more I want to execute him," Carlton muttered.

"I'm right there with you," replied Mabel. "And we might not have any other choice. It's not like we can safely turn the guy loose in the community, not while Ricardo is alive. Let's take care of that, then see how he's doing."

She pointed across the room at the basement door, which sported a big STAY OUT sign. Carlton couldn't shake the feeling that it looked like the door to a teenager's bedroom.

"The door to the basement will be locked and reinforced with steel bars," Mabel told him. "We'll have to..."

She shut her mouth and stared. Carlton had walked across the room and pushed on the door, and it swung open as if one of the vampire's servants had forgotten to lock the master in when he went downstairs for the day.

"Something's going on," she commented. "I don't trust this."

Carlton knew what she meant. "I'll go first, then. You cover me from behind."

He went down the staircase one careful step after another, gun in his right hand and flashlight in his left. The basement had small windows, but they'd been painted black and covered with thick velvet curtains. They could only see what they were looking at when they pointed their flashlights directly at it.

It soon became obvious that they were not alone. In his training classes, Carlton had been told about "feeding dolls," captive humans kept on hand by a master vampire to be drained slowly, then discarded.

Ricardo's three feeding dolls were beautiful young men picked up in the gay clubs of South Beach. At one point, they'd been toned and tanned, muscular guys who would have had their pick of partners on the dance floor.

After nights of being drained by Ricardo and his friends, they looked like hollow gourds rather than human beings. Chained to the ceiling by their wrists, they dangled limply, their heads hanging like broken toys.

"Hang on!" Mabel called, "We'll get you out of here!"

Carlton wasn't so sure. There was something about the way they hung. They didn't look like they'd be getting out.

He walked over to the first one, a young Cuban. "Hey, man. We're here to help."

The man didn't respond. Carlton pushed up his chin and saw the gaping wound in his neck. This wasn't the work of a vampire. Someone had practically cut his head off. Someone had been there before them.

"Look, Mabel."

She turned, her eyes big. "Check the others."

They were all the same. Someone had come into this place without the guards seeing them and nearly decapitated all three of Ricardo's feeding dolls.

Who would be cruel enough to do such a thing?

"Carlton, get over here," Mabel told him.

He came running, and the first thing he saw was Ricardo's arm. It had been severed from his body by a sharp blade, then tossed in a corner.

There was a hand a few feet away, and a lower leg. Then they saw a limbless torso.

Someone had cut Ricardo into a dozen pieces and written words on the basement wall in blood.

A New Order Rises.

Below the bloody words, Ricardo's severed head stared at the world. From the look in his eyes, the last thing he'd seen had been more terrifying than he was. His head was impaled on a long, ornate knife with a chunk of amber topping the hilt.

Mabel sighed. "It looks like you and your team are going to have competition."

THE STORY CONTINUES

The story continues with book two, *At All Costs,* available at Amazon.

Claim your copy today!

AUTHOR NOTES

MARCH 15, 2023

First, thank you for not only reading this story but also these author notes in the back. Your dedication to my storytelling is much appreciated.

The Veil: A Not-So-Fictitious Scenario

As I was concocting this urban fantasy, my mind kept wandering to a hypothetical situation: What if "The Veil" was real? What if supernatural beings and mystical powers were indeed lurking in the shadows of our world? How would governments react, and what lengths would they go to keep it hidden?

Now, bear with me as I put on my conspiracy-theorist hat and dive into this thought experiment. (It's made of tinfoil, if you wanted to know.)

Governments have a vested interest in maintaining order and control, ensuring that their citizens remain within the confines of their established systems. The existence of supernatural forces would disrupt this order, creating chaos and panic among the population. So, it's not difficult to imagine that they would do everything in their power to keep "The Veil" hidden.

First, they would establish secret organizations tasked with monitoring and controlling supernatural activities. These organizations would be given unlimited resources and jurisdiction to operate in the shadows, away from public scrutiny. Their primary objective: to maintain "The Veil" and prevent any supernatural incidents from reaching the public eye.

Second, these organizations would work tirelessly to discredit any evidence of supernatural phenomena. They would manipulate the media, spreading disinformation and promoting skepticism. Any individuals who claim to have encountered supernatural beings or events would be labeled as delusional or frauds.

Lastly (Finally? Thirdly?), the government would keep a tight leash on any individuals with supernatural abilities. These gifted individuals would either be recruited into their secret organizations or monitored closely to ensure they didn't pose a threat to the established order.

The idea of "The Veil" existing in our world is fascinating. As a writer, it allows me to explore themes of secrecy, power dynamics, and the lengths to which governments might go to maintain control. It makes for an excellent urban fantasy setting. And who knows, maybe there's a grain of truth to it after all!

But enough about hypothetical scenarios. Let's get back to the real world, where our biggest concern is finding the perfect Chili recipe, not accidentally stumbling upon a supernatural secret war.

As always, thank you for joining me on this wild ride. I

hope you enjoyed the story and these somewhat outlandish author notes. Talk to you in the next book!

Ad Aeternitatem,

Michael 'Tin Hat' Anderle

If you want to, you can read a couple of short stories that I am sharing in my STORIES with Michael Anderle newsletter here: https://michael.beehiiv.com/

CONNECT WITH THE AUTHOR

Connect with Michael Anderle

Website: http://lmbpn.com

Email List: https://michael.beehiiv.com/

https://www.facebook.com/LMBPNPublishing

https://twitter.com/MichaelAnderle

https://www.instagram.com/lmbpn_publishing/

https://www.bookbub.com/authors/michael-anderle

BOOKS BY MICHAEL ANDERLE

Sign up for the LMBPN email list to be notified of new releases and special deals!

https://lmbpn.com/email/

For a complete list of books by Michael Anderle, please visit:

www.lmbpn.com/ma-books/